The THIRD FORM at St CLARE'S

Have you read these other great books in the *Enid Blyton* collection?

St Clare's

The Twins at St Clare's
The O'Sullivan Twins
Summer Term at St Clare's
Second Form at St Clare's
The Third Form at St Clare's (by Pamela Cox)
Kitty at St Clare's (by Pamela Cox)
Claudine at St Clare's
Fifth Formers of St Clare's
The Sixth Form at St Clare's (by Pamela Cox)

Malory Towers

First Term at Malory Towers
Second Form at Malory Towers
Third Year at Malory Towers
Upper Fourth at Malory Towers
In the Fifth at Malory Towers
Last Term at Malory Towers

The Mysteries

The Mystery of the Burnt Cottage
The Mystery of the Disappearing Cat
The Mystery of the Secret Room
The Mystery of the Spiteful Letters
The Mystery of the Missing Necklace
The Mystery of the Hidden House
The Mystery of the Pantomime Cat
The Mystery of the Invisible Thief
The Mystery of the Vanished Prince
The Mystery of the Strange Bundle
The Mystery of Holly Lane
The Mystery of Tally-Ho Cottage
The Mystery of the Missing Man
The Mystery of the Strange Messages
The Mystery of Banshee Towers

Collect them all NOW!

Enid Blyton

The THIRD FORM at St CLARE'S

Written by
Pamela Cox

EGMONT

Enid Blyton

EGMONT
We bring stories to life

First published in Great Britain 2000
This edition published in 2014 by Egmont UK Limited
The Yellow Building, 1 Nicholas Road
London W11 4AN

Text copyright © 2000 Hodder & Stoughton
Illustration copyright © 2014 Hodder & Stoughton
ENID BLYTON ® Copyright © 2014 Hodder & Stoughton

ISBN 978 1 4052 7286 5

1 3 5 7 9 10 8 6 4 2

www.egmont.co.uk

26839/21

A CIP catalogue record for this title is available from the British Library.

Printed and bound in Great Britain by the CPI Group.

Stay safe online. Any website addresses listed in this book are correct
at the time of going to print. However, Egmont is not responsible for content
hosted by third parties. Please be aware that online content can be subject to
change and websites can contain content that is unsuitable for children.
We advise that all children are supervised when using the internet.

EGMONT

Our story began over a century ago, when seventeen-year-old
Egmont Harald Petersen found a coin in the street. He was on
his way to buy a flyswatter, a small hand-operated printing
machine that he then set up in his tiny apartment.

The coin brought him such good luck that today Egmont has
offices in over 30 countries around the world. And that lucky
coin is still kept at the company's head offices in Denmark.

Contents

1	Back to school	1
2	Another new girl . . .	7
3	. . . And a head girl	14
4	A very important meeting	22
5	Settling down	30
6	A wonderful day	39
7	An announcement – and a plan	47
8	A ghostly trick	54
9	Carlotta in hot water	62
10	A birthday party	70
11	Half-term	77
12	A bad day for Rachel	84
13	Another row	91
14	An apology – and a birthday	99
15	Midnight feast	108
16	A very angry third form	116
17	A hard time for Fern	124
18	Fern is foolish	131
19	Bad news – and good news	139
20	Things are sorted out	147
21	A marvellous play	155
20	Home for the holidays	162

Back to school

'Not long now and we'll be back at St Clare's,' said Isabel O'Sullivan, glancing out of the car window.

'Yes. It feels as though we've been away for *months*, not just a few weeks,' said her twin, Pat.

'Anyone would think the two of you positively disliked coming home for the holidays!' said their mother from the driving seat.

'Oh, Mum, of course we love being at home!' cried Pat. 'It's just . . .' Then, in the mirror, she caught the twinkle in her mother's eye and laughed.

'I wonder who will be head of the form this term?' mused Isabel.

'One of you two, perhaps?' suggested their friend, Carlotta Brown. She lived several miles away from the twins and had been delighted when Mrs O'Sullivan had telephoned to offer her a ride back to school. Her father was away, and the girl hadn't been looking forward to making the journey in the company of her rather strict, disapproving grandmother. 'It certainly won't be me,' she went on now with a laugh. 'Miss Theobald thinks that I'm still too wild and irresponsible.'

'Perhaps she will choose you for that very reason,'

suggested Mrs O'Sullivan. 'A little responsibility might do you good and calm you down a bit.'

Carlotta looked doubtful. She wasn't at all sure that she *wanted* to be calmed down!

'I hope it's not you or me, Pat,' said Isabel. 'I'd be just green with envy if you were head girl. Yet I'd feel dreadful about you being left out if I was chosen!'

Pat laughed. 'Yes, that's exactly how I feel.'

'I shouldn't be surprised if it's Hilary again,' said Carlotta. 'She's certainly had plenty of experience and she's always done a marvellous job.'

'In that case, perhaps it's time someone else had a chance,' put in the twins' mother. 'Hilary's already proved that she can lead and accept responsibility.'

'Mm. Janet, perhaps?' said Isabel. 'Certainly not Bobby! When it comes to being wild and irresponsible, there's not much to choose between her and you, Carlotta!'

Carlotta grinned broadly at this then, suddenly, she gave a gasp, her dark eyes widening. 'Look – over there! Mrs O'Sullivan, would you mind stopping for a moment?'

The twins' mother pulled in to the grass verge, while Pat and Isabel turned their heads to see what Carlotta was so excited about.

'Why, someone has bought the Oaks!' exclaimed Pat. 'And they've turned it into riding stables. Wonderful!'

The Oaks was a large and very beautiful house a short distance from St Clare's, set in several acres of green fields. It had been standing empty and neglected for some time, but now the front door was freshly painted and the windows gleaming. More importantly as far as the girls were concerned, a series of jumps was set up in the adjoining field, and they could see a girl on a beautiful white horse cantering round.

'May we stop and take a look, Mum?' asked Isabel eagerly.

'Yes, we've plenty of time,' replied Mrs O'Sullivan. 'I'll wait in the car and read the newspaper.'

The three girls scrambled out of the car, going straight to the fence that bordered the field. The girl on horseback spotted them and immediately rode across, long brown hair streaming out from beneath her riding hat.

'Hallo there!' she called out with a friendly smile. 'Come to have a look at Snowdrop here?'

'If you don't mind,' answered Carlotta, liking the look of the horse at once. 'Hey, aren't you a beauty?' This last remark was addressed to Snowdrop, whose snow-white neck she at once began to stroke.

'You wouldn't be St Clare's girls, by any chance?' asked their new acquaintance, dismounting.

'We most certainly would,' said Carlotta. 'And, I can promise you, you'll be seeing several of us here regularly – me for one!'

The girl laughed. 'We might be seeing more of one another than you think! My cousin and I are starting in the third form – as day girls! Miss Theobald has agreed to take us at reduced fees. In return, my parents have agreed on special terms for any pupil who wishes to ride here. Oh, I'm Libby Francis, by the way.'

Delighted at this turn of events, the twins and Carlotta introduced themselves, Pat remarking, 'We're in the third too!'

'What a bit of luck!' exclaimed Libby. 'I'm afraid we won't be with you for very long, though. Fern – that's my cousin – is staying with us for a few months whilst her parents are abroad. And I'm due to go to America on an exchange scheme in the autumn.'

Just then a movement at the other end of the field caught everyone's eyes and they saw a girl and boy approach the gate there.

'Fern!' called out Libby. 'Over here!'

The girl opened the gate and began to walk across the field, while the boy turned away abruptly and made for the stables.

'My brother, Will,' explained Libby. 'He goes to day school in Lowchester, a few miles away.' She lowered her voice and went on, 'Fern absolutely idolizes him and makes a prize nuisance of herself hanging round him all the time. Will can't bear girls – apart from me – and he thinks that she's just too silly for words!'

'I'll bet he wasn't too pleased when he found out that she was coming to stay,' laughed Isabel.

'That's putting it mildly!' said Libby. 'You see, it all started when we were kids and I pulled the head off Fern's favourite doll. Will fixed it and, ever since, she's treated him like some kind of hero.'

Fern looked a little like a doll herself, thought Isabel as the girl approached. A very pretty china doll, with her pink and white complexion, golden hair and wide, blue eyes. Unlike her cousin, who was casually dressed for riding, Fern wore a pretty summer dress and high-heeled sandals, on which she teetered and stumbled over the uneven ground. Really, thought Pat, she looks as if she's going to a garden party!

'Fern, come and meet Carlotta, Pat and Isabel, from St Clare's,' said her cousin. 'We're all going to be in the third together.'

Fern said hallo in a high, pretty voice, and Pat noticed that she kept a cautious distance from Libby's horse, shying away nervously every time the animal tossed its head.

'Do you ride, Fern?' she asked.

'Oh, no!' The girl shuddered and shook her golden curls. 'Horses frighten me to death! I have other interests.'

Libby grinned fondly at her cousin and said impishly, 'Yes, Fern's interested in her hair, her nails, her clothes . . .'

Fern turned red and gave Libby a little push, while the twins exchanged grins. Winking at Carlotta, Isabel said smoothly, 'Our cousin Alison will be in the third too – and her interests are exactly the same as yours! I just bet the two of you will get on like a house on fire!'

'Oh, that would be great!' breathed Fern, her big blue eyes growing even rounder. 'To have a friend who likes the same things as I do.'

'Well, you and Alison are welcome to your fashions and fancy hair-dos,' said Libby bluntly. 'Give me my horses any day! How about you, twins? Are you interested in riding?'

'We've had a few lessons,' answered Pat. 'But we're not in Carlotta's league. She used to ride in a circus, you know.'

Libby looked at the dark girl with interest, exclaiming and pressing her to tell all about her life in the circus. Even Fern dropped her sophisticated pose and came out of her cloud of self-absorption to ask Carlotta several interested questions.

Just then the girls heard Mrs O'Sullivan calling and Carlotta, reluctant to leave, pulled a face. 'Back to school for us!'

'We don't start until tomorrow morning,' said Libby. 'It must be such fun, all of you being together all the time.'

'Yes, we have some good times,' laughed Pat. 'And we try to fit in a midnight feast each term!'

'Midnight feasts! How marvellous that sounds,' sighed Libby wistfully. 'But Fern and I will be here at home each night, and shan't be able to join in anything like that.'

Carlotta grinned wickedly. 'I wouldn't be too sure. At St Clare's, *anything* is possible!'

2

Another new girl . . .

On the short drive from the stables to St Clare's, the girls chattered non-stop about the two day girls, thrilled that they had been the first to meet them.

'What a piece of news to tell the others!' said Pat.

'Yes, and what a term it's going to be,' Carlotta sighed happily. 'I don't know that I'll have time to fit any school work in. I shall be too busy riding!'

The twins laughed and Isabel said, 'Libby seems a good sort. I don't know that I'm too keen on Fern, though.'

'Me neither,' agreed Carlotta with a grimace. 'Still, with any luck we should be able to push her off on to Alison.'

'Oh, yes, Alison will think she's just too wonderful for words,' chuckled Pat. 'No doubt she'll spend the whole term in Fern's pocket.'

But the girls were in for a surprise once they reached St Clare's and had said goodbye to Mrs O'Sullivan. For there in the big hall was the twins' cousin, already arm in arm with another new girl. This one seemed the complete opposite of Fern, being dark and rather serious looking.

'Twins! Carlotta!' called out Alison, pulling her new friend forward. 'Enjoyed the holidays? Come and meet our new girl, Rachel Denman.'

The three girls introduced themselves and Rachel inclined her head graciously. The reason for her rather haughty manner was made clear when Alison said in hushed tones, 'Rachel is the daughter of Sir Robert and Lady Helen Denman, the well-known actors. What do you think of that?'

'Wow!' exclaimed Pat, very much impressed despite the fact that she hadn't taken to Rachel at all. 'Isabel and I saw one of their films at the pictures during the holidays and they were both just marvellous. It must be wonderful to have that kind of talent. Do you mean to follow in their footsteps?'

'Naturally I intend to become an actress,' answered the girl sharply, as though surprised that Pat should ask such a foolish question. 'Until recently I went to drama school in London.'

She had a beautiful speaking voice, low pitched, yet clear as crystal. Due to her drama coaching, no doubt, thought Isabel.

'What made you decide to leave and come to St Clare's?' she asked.

'My parents feel strongly that one must experience *real* life to be able to inject true emotion into one's acting,' she explained loftily. 'So for the next year I'm just to be an ordinary schoolgirl, like the rest of you.'

The twins and Carlotta stared at her hard. Her condescending manner really put their backs up. As though sensing that the others didn't think much of Rachel, and fearing that they might say something cutting, Alison said hastily, 'I'd better take you to Matron, then we'll see which dormitory we're in. I do hope we're together.'

'I suppose we "ordinary" mortals ought to pop along to Matron too,' remarked Carlotta as Alison and Rachel walked away. But before they had a chance, the girls heard their names called and turned to see Janet Robins and Bobby Ellis walking towards them.

'Hallo! I see you've met the actress. What do you think of her?' asked Janet with a wry grin.

'So good of her to come down and live among us little people,' said Bobby, a scornful look on her freckled face. 'My word, if she puts on her high and mighty airs with me she'll learn all about true emotion, all right!'

The others laughed. Rachel was the kind of girl who brought out the worst in the forthright Bobby. She just couldn't bear airs and graces, as she called them.

'Trust your cousin to latch on to her,' remarked Janet drily.

Pat gave a chuckle. 'Don't be surprised if Alison changes her affections tomorrow, Janet. We've two more new girls starting then – and one of them is just Alison's cup of tea!'

'Hallo, what's this?' The dark, good-looking Hilary Wentworth came up, accompanied by Doris Elward. 'Who's Alison's cup of tea? Tell us!'

'Hilary!' cried the girls. 'And Doris!'

'Just arrived back?'

'Good to see you both again!'

Once the girls had greeted each other, Janet nudged

Pat and said impatiently, 'Go on! Let's hear all about these new girls.'

So Pat, with much eager assistance from Isabel and Carlotta, told the listening girls all about Libby and Fern, extremely gratified at the reaction their news produced.

'Day girls! How thrilling!'

'And riding stables right on our doorstep. Brilliant!'

'Looks as if it's shaping up to be a fab term!' remarked Hilary. 'And we've got the glorious summer weather too, which means plenty of tennis and swimming. Come on, let's hurry along to Matron and give her our things. If we're quick there might just be time to take a look at the swimming-pool before tea. I know we won't be able to go in, but just looking at that clear blue water lapping at the sides makes me feel all nice and summery!'

Everyone agreed with this and, picking up their night-cases, they sped along to Matron's room. But they never did get to visit the swimming-pool, caught up in the first-day bustle of unpacking, finding their dormitories, greeting girls, mistresses – and Miss Theobald, the wise, kindly head mistress, of course. Then the bell sounded for tea, and before the girls knew what had happened, the day was over and it was bedtime.

Alison, to her great disappointment, wasn't in the same dormitory as Rachel, but had been allocated a bed next to Mirabel Unwin. This didn't thrill her at all as Mirabel was rumoured to snore loudly! She sought out Mirabel's best friend, the quiet little Gladys, who was in Rachel's dormitory, and whispered, 'Gladys! How about you and I swapping places? Then you can be next to Mirabel.'

'Why, that's very kind of you, Alison!' exclaimed Gladys, quite unaware that Alison had her own reasons for wanting to change places. 'But aren't we supposed to ask Matron if we want to move dormitories?'

'Yes, you are,' said Hilary, coming up with Janet and overhearing this. 'What's up, Gladys? Do you want to go in with Mirabel?'

'Well, it was Alison's idea,' replied Gladys, anxious to give credit where it was due.

'Really,' said Hilary drily. 'I wonder why?'

Alison blushed and said hastily, 'I was only thinking of Gladys, and how nice it would be for her to be next to Mirabel.'

'And I suppose this has nothing to do with the fact that your precious Rachel is in the other dormitory?' put in Janet with a grin.

'Alison, if you want to change with Gladys, kindly make your request through Matron tomorrow,' Hilary said with calm authority. 'Now it's bedtime, so I suggest you go and get ready – quickly!'

'Spoken like a true head girl,' said Janet with a chuckle as Alison, rather sullenly, went into her dormitory.

Hilary laughed. 'Perhaps, but I'm not head girl.'

'You will be tomorrow,' said Janet confidently. 'Once Miss Adams has made the announcement.'

'I don't think so,' responded Hilary thoughtfully. 'I overheard Miss Jenks saying last term that she thought it was time someone else had a chance.'

'Really? Won't you mind standing down?' asked Janet curiously.

'Not at all,' answered Hilary. 'I thoroughly enjoyed being head girl and appreciated what an honour it was. But it's a big responsibility and I'll be quite happy to sit back and let someone else take it this term.' She paused and looked thoughtfully at Janet. 'You, perhaps?'

'Never!' Janet dismissed this with a laugh. 'I'm too fond of jokes and tricks to make a good head girl.'

'Yes, but you're also a born leader and a strong character,' pointed out Hilary. 'Anyway, we'll find out tomorrow.'

'Yes,' said Janet slowly, Hilary's words making her think.

The girls, worn out by their long journeys and the excitement of the day, fell asleep quickly. All except two of them. One was Rachel Denman, who lay staring miserably into the dark, aware that she had made a bad start with the girls.

It's all so very different from my drama school, she thought unhappily. Only Alison seems to like me. Still, I suppose that's my fault for getting on my high horse. But somehow I just find myself going all defensive and can't seem to help it. Sighing heavily, the girl turned over in her bed. If only they knew it was my stupid pride making me act like that, she thought. But I can't bring myself to tell them the truth.

The other girl was Janet, who lay awake for a very different reason – excitement! Until that conversation with Hilary, it had never occurred to her that she might be in the running for head of the form. But now that she

12

came to think about it, why shouldn't she be? After all, she, Hilary and Doris had been at St Clare's longer than any of the others. Well, Hilary had had her turn, and as for Doris – Janet grinned to herself – Doris, the duffer, would run a mile if the honour was offered to her. There wasn't an ounce of conceit in Janet's nature, but the more she thought about it, the more she saw herself as the obvious choice for head girl. At last she drifted off to sleep, her thoughts pleasant. Tomorrow . . . she thought drowsily. Tomorrow she would know.

3

. . . And a head girl

When the laughing, chattering stream of third formers made their way into the classroom after breakfast next morning, Fern and Libby were already there, looking out of the big window at the gardens. They turned as the girls entered and Pat called out, 'Hi! You two are keen!'

'We wanted to make a good impression on our first day,' said Libby with her ready grin. 'Fern's been up since the crack of dawn doing her hair and nails!'

Fern blushed and Alison, looking at the pretty, dainty girl with approval, stepped forward.

'Fern!' she said with her charming smile. 'What a pretty name!'

Fern smiled back, recognizing at once in Alison many of the traits that were in her own character.

'You must be Alison,' she said. 'The twins have told me all about you.'

Alison looked rather doubtful at this, casting a suspicious glance at her cousins, who were introducing Libby to the others. Evidently, though, they hadn't said anything bad about her to Fern, for the girl seemed only too eager to make friends. Soon she and Alison were in the thick of a discussion on the latest fashions.

'Two feather-heads together,' murmured Carlotta with a grin. 'Rachel isn't going to be too pleased. Where is she, by the way?'

'She left her pencil-case in the dormitory and had to go back for it,' said Bobby. 'Here she comes now.'

Indeed, Rachel looked extremely put out when she walked in and saw her new friend engrossed in conversation with someone else. Alison spotted her and beckoned her over, wondering how Rachel would feel about making up a threesome with Fern. Alas, there was no time to find out, for Doris, standing guard at the door, hissed, 'Hush! Miss Adams is coming!'

Immediately the chattering ceased, the girls standing straight, as a short, dark young woman entered. Miss Adams, the third-form mistress, looked plain and rather dour – until she smiled, and then her whole face lit up. She smiled now, saying, 'Good morning, girls. Find yourselves desks as quickly as possible, please.'

There was the usual scramble for places in the back row, only the three new girls standing aside and waiting – as was the custom – for the others to bag their seats first.

Alison chose a middle-row desk by the window, then both Fern and Rachel made a beeline for the vacant one next to her. They reached it neck and neck, Fern placing her bag on the desk at precisely the same time as Rachel sat down on the chair.

'I was here first!' they cried in unison.

Doris nudged Libby and grinned.

'I put my bag on the desk before you sat down!' insisted Fern indignantly.

'Well, I reached the chair first, so it's mine!' said Rachel, equally determined, as she glared at her rival.

'What it is to be popular,' murmured Bobby, seated directly behind a red-faced Alison.

'Move your things!' demanded Rachel arrogantly.

'I shan't!' refused Fern, blue eyes sparkling with anger. '*You* can just move yourself!'

'Excuse me!' boomed Miss Adams, stern eyes fixed on the two quarrelling girls. 'I was under the impression that I was teaching the third form at a senior school, not a kindergarten class. And it's customary, young lady, to stand when you are being addressed by a mistress!'

Blushing furiously, Rachel shot to her feet, keeping one hand possessively on the back of the chair, as though afraid that Fern would snatch it from her.

'And you!' Miss Adams's sharp eyes switched to Fern, who had been smirking triumphantly. 'Are you wearing *nail polish*?'

Quaking, Fern stammered, 'It – it's only a clear one, Miss Adams.'

'Kindly remove it at the earliest opportunity!' the mistress ordered sternly. 'And never let me catch you wearing it in class again.'

Humiliated, and aware of the wide grins of the rest of the class – with the exception of Alison, who looked as though she wanted to sink through the floor – Fern pursed her pretty mouth. Even her own cousin thought it was hilarious, she realized, glaring at Libby, who was clinging helplessly to Doris.

'Now, the two of you have precisely ten seconds to sit down, or you will stand outside!' barked Miss Adams, looking at her watch. 'Ten . . . nine . . . eight . . .'

'Oh, move along, Rachel!' snapped Alison with unusual impatience. So much for her ideas of a threesome!

'Fern, you come and sit here by the window, and I'll go in the middle.'

'Poor Alison,' whispered Doris. 'She's like the meat in a sandwich!'

Libby giggled then, seeing the mistress's eye on her, turned it into a long cough.

'Now, if everyone's settled, perhaps we can get on?' said Miss Adams with sarcasm.

Immediately, everyone fell silent and sat up straight, wiping the grins from their faces as Miss Adams continued. 'I'm sure that all of you are keen to know who will be head of the form. Miss Theobald and I both consulted Miss Jenks, as you were in her form last year and she obviously knows you better than I do at this stage. There were a couple of you in the running and it was a very close thing but, after much consideration, our choice is . . . Carlotta Brown!' There was a moment's silence then the form erupted, cheering and yelling.

'Good for you, Carlotta!'

'Yes, well done!'

Carlotta stared blankly round. At last she said, 'Pardon?'

'Carlotta,' explained Hilary patiently. 'You're head of the form.'

'Who, me?' said Carlotta, eyes widening. 'No, there's some mistake.'

Miss Adams laughed at the girl's air of disbelief and said, 'There's no mistake, Carlotta.'

'Well!' exclaimed the girl, astonished. 'I really don't know what to say! It's a real honour and I'll do my best to live up to it, you can be sure.'

So Mrs O'Sullivan's prediction had come true, she realized, her head in a whirl. This was the last thing she had expected!

As Miss Adams had said, it had been a close thing. Mam'zelle had entered the staff common-room as Miss Theobald and the two mistresses were discussing the matter, giving a shriek of protest when she heard Carlotta's name mentioned.

'Ah, *non*! That Carlotta, she is too wild! She will lead the third formers into all kinds of scratches!'

'Scratches? Oh, you mean scrapes, Mam'zelle!' Miss Theobald had laughed. 'What do you think of Janet, then?'

The Frenchwoman's sloe-black eyes became sombre as she shook her head gravely, sitting down at the table with the others. 'She is too fond of the trick and the joke. It is not dignified in a head girl!'

'Both girls have their faults,' remarked Miss Jenks thoughtfully. 'Carlotta is inclined to be reckless and hot tempered, while Janet can be a little too sharp tongued and lacking in tact. Yet both are strong, determined characters and have the makings of leaders.'

'I agree,' said Miss Theobald. 'And neither of them has any mean, petty faults. I think a little responsibility might do them the world of good.'

'But how do we choose between them?' asked Miss Adams.

'I propose that we make Carlotta head girl for this term, and let Janet have her chance next term,' replied the head. 'What do you all think?'

'An excellent idea!' said Miss Jenks decidedly. Miss Adams nodded in agreement.

'*Mais oui*!' cried Mam'zelle, her earlier comments on the two girls suddenly forgotten as she was swept along on a tide of enthusiasm. 'It is as you say, Miss Theobald! It will be so, so good for the dear girls! Ah, what fine leaders they will make.'

Miss Theobald and the two mistresses found it hard to hide their smiles. How well they knew Mam'zelle's little ways! In a few moments she would have convinced herself that the whole idea had been hers, thought Miss Jenks.

'We're agreed, then,' said Miss Adams briskly. 'Carlotta Brown is to be head girl this term, and Janet Robins next.'

What a pity that the mistresses didn't let Janet in on the plan!

She, to her dismay, was feeling extremely jealous, a novel and unpleasant experience for her. Yet the girl liked Carlotta immensely and, even in the midst of her own disappointment, wanted to feel pleased for her friend and back her up. So Janet nobly swallowed her feelings, fixed a smile to her face and called out, 'That's marvellous, Carlotta! You'll make a wonderful head girl!'

'Thanks! I certainly hope so,' answered Carlotta, still feeling quite overwhelmed.

'I'm sure you will,' said Miss Adams. 'Now, I've another piece of news that I'm sure will interest you all. Miss Theobald would like the third to produce an end-of-term play, to which the parents are to be invited.'

The girls sat up straight, exchanging excited glances. This was great news! Gladys put up her hand to ask, 'What kind of play, Miss Adams?'

'That's entirely up to you,' answered the mistress. 'It's quite literally your show – from the script, to the costumes and scenery. Naturally, the mistresses, including myself, will be on hand to give you any help or advice required, but the final decisions will all be yours.'

And judging from the babble of noise that broke out, there would be no lack of ideas or enthusiasm!

Miss Adams rapped on the desk with a ruler and said loudly, 'Well, I'm delighted that you are all so keen, but I suggest you wait until break-time to discuss the matter. In the meantime, I'm afraid, we have to get down to the more mundane task of making out timetables.'

The girls did their best to concentrate, but how the morning crawled by! Then, at last, it was break and the third form found a secluded corner of the playground where they could discuss this exciting news.

'There's no time to hold a proper meeting now,' said Hilary, taking charge. 'So I vote we hold one after tea . . .'

Her voice trailed off as Isabel nudged her and nodded in Carlotta's direction.

'Carlotta, I'm sorry!' she apologized, blushing. 'Old habits die hard, I'm afraid. But this is your job now.'

'No need to apologize,' laughed Carlotta. 'I haven't got used to the idea of being head girl myself yet! Well, as Hilary says, the best thing would be to hold a meeting in the common-room after tea . . .'

'Hold on!' interrupted Libby. 'Fern and I go home at tea-time, remember? We don't want to be left out.'

'Oh, yes, I forgot!' exclaimed Carlotta. 'Will your parents let you come back to school for the meeting? It will still be light when we finish and you don't have far to walk.'

'I don't see why not,' replied Libby. 'We'll ask them as soon as we get home.'

'Good! All right, girls, after tea it is,' said Carlotta, grinning round. 'Put your thinking caps on, everyone, and be sure to bring plenty of ideas with you.'

A very important meeting

Carlotta perched on the edge of a table in the common-room and looked round at the third formers, all of them eagerly waiting for the meeting to begin.

'I'm really looking forward to this,' said Isabel, her eyes sparkling.

'Me too,' agreed Hilary. 'We'll all have to work hard and do our best to get things just perfect, especially as our parents are coming. We want to make them proud of us.'

'I suppose you'll be auditioning for one of the leading roles, Gladys?' said Bobby.

'I don't know about that,' said the quiet little Gladys with her usual modesty. 'It all depends on what kind of play we decide to do and whether or not I'm suitable.'

'You'd be suitable for *any* part,' Pat told her warmly. 'It's just amazing the way you can transform yourself into any character you choose.'

Gladys was a very fine little actress indeed and the girls had discovered her talent quite by chance, half-way through her first term at St Clare's. Before that she had been a miserable, timid little character with no friends. Then Mirabel had unexpectedly taken the girl under her wing after learning that Gladys's mother was seriously ill in hospital and that that was why the girl was so unhappy.

Mirabel's friendship had made a big difference to Gladys, bringing her out of her shell. It had been Mirabel who discovered that Gladys could act and had persuaded her to perform for the others; Mirabel who had been a tower of strength when the girl's mother had undergone a serious operation; Mirabel who had rejoiced with her when her mother made a full recovery. And now it was Mirabel who said loyally, 'Pat's right. You're easily the best actress St Clare's has ever had.'

Rachel had been listening to this with a rather strange, frozen expression and Alison, fearing that the girl might be offended at her own talents being over-looked, said reassuringly, 'Gladys *is* very good, but I'm sure that you will be able to give her a few pointers. With your background you're certain to get one of the leading parts.'

Bobby and Janet, standing nearby, caught the end of this and grinned at Alison's gushing tone.

Then Rachel gave a little laugh and said, 'Sorry to disappoint you, Alison, but I'm not interested in having a leading role – or *any* role for that matter.'

This was too much for Bobby, who whipped round and said scornfully, 'I suppose a mere school play is quite beneath you! Well, Rachel, this might not be the kind of grand production that you're used to, but it means a lot to us.'

'You bet it does!' called out some of the others, glaring at the new girl.

'Quite frankly,' went on Bobby, 'I think we'll manage very well without you.'

Completely taken aback by Bobby's contemptuous tone and the hostile stares around her, Rachel turned red with dismay. She *didn't* think the play was beneath her! She hadn't meant it like that at all! But what was the point of trying to defend herself? Every time she opened her mouth these days, things seemed to come out sounding all wrong. And the third formers seemed determined to think the very worst of her.

Fortunately Mirabel created a diversion then, calling out impatiently, 'Can't we get started? Gladys and I were hoping to get some tennis practice in before prep!'

'Libby and Fern haven't arrived yet,' pointed out Carlotta. 'We'll give them five more minutes, then start without them.'

Thankfully, as Mirabel was growing extremely restless, the two day girls arrived a moment later.

'Sorry we're late,' said Libby ruefully. 'What's happened? Have we missed much?'

'We haven't started yet,' said Carlotta, clapping her hands for silence. 'All right, girls, let's begin. Now, does anyone have any thoughts on what sort of a play we should do?'

Everyone did, and a dozen voices cried out at once.

'An historical drama!'

'No, comedy!'

'Better still, how about a musical comedy?' suggested Bobby. 'That would be brilliant!'

'Yes, but it might be a little ambitious,' said Isabel doubtfully. 'If it's to be all our own work, that would mean we would have to write songs and music scores, as well as a script, and none of us has any great talent in that direction.'

'I think you're right,' agreed Carlotta. 'So, that leaves us with comedy or drama.'

'I'd love to do a costume drama,' said Fern who, to Rachel's annoyance, had made straight for Alison. 'At my last school I played a princess in our play and the dress I wore was simply beautiful. White satin, with lace and . . .'

'There is a little more to acting than simply dressing up, you know,' Rachel interrupted cuttingly.

'I was speaking to Alison,' said Fern pointedly, glaring at Rachel before turning her back on the girl.

'Well, it's very rude of you to speak to *anyone* when Carlotta is trying to get on with the meeting,' said Hilary bluntly. 'For Heaven's sake, shut up and do let's get on!'

Flushing hotly, Fern subsided and Carlotta continued, 'Whatever kind of play we decide to put on, we're going to need a really good script. Does anyone think they can write one?'

'I wouldn't mind having a bash at a comedy,' replied Doris, who had a marvellous sense of humour and could send the girls into fits of laughter with her wonderful gift for mimicry.

'And I'd rather like to try my hand at drama,' volunteered Hilary, who was excellent at English.

Several more girls spoke up too and Carlotta said with

a grin, 'Well, I was afraid no one would want this particular job, but it seems that we're a form of budding playwrights! I think the fairest thing would be if everyone leaves their finished scripts on my desk – without names attached, so that I can't be accused of any favouritism. Then I'll ask Miss Adams to read through them with me and, between us, we'll pick the best one.'

'We're going to have to get a move on,' said Doris. 'Until we have a play, we can't dish out parts, paint scenery or make costumes.'

'Then we'd better set a deadline,' said Carlotta decidedly. 'All completed scripts to be on my desk – or Miss Adams's – by five o'clock, three weeks from today.'

'Three weeks!' exclaimed Hilary. 'Considering none of us has ever attempted to write a play before, that's quite a task.'

'I know, but, as Doris says, we need to get things moving,' replied Carlotta. 'If we leave it any longer, we shan't have time to rehearse properly, and that would never do! I'm sure we all want this to be a big success.'

There was a chorus of agreement at this. 'There is one thing we can do without a script,' called out Bobby. 'And that's choose a director. It'll have to be someone who can lead and keep us all in order.'

'Carlotta!' cried Doris. 'After all, she's head girl and she can probably do with a bit of practice at bossing us all around!'

'Thank you, Doris!' laughed Carlotta. 'But I don't think I ought to take control just because I'm head of the form!

Perhaps someone else would like to have a bash?'

'I think Janet would make an excellent director,' said Bobby. 'What do you say, Janet?'

Janet suddenly thought that directing would be just the kind of challenge she enjoyed – and it would make up for her disappointment at not being head girl. 'I wouldn't mind giving it a try,' she said. 'Provided the majority agree.'

'Well, there's only one way to find out,' said Pat. 'And that's to take a vote. Does anyone have any paper?'

'I've a notebook here,' said Alison, tearing off some sheets and beginning to hand them round.

'Half a minute!' called Hilary. 'The three new girls shouldn't vote, because they don't really know Janet or Carlotta yet.'

'And Janet and I can't vote either,' said Carlotta. 'So that leaves the rest of you. An odd number – that's lucky!'

Hilary collected the votes and counted them – which didn't take very long at all. Then she cleared her throat and said, 'Well, that couldn't have been much closer! The winner, by one vote, is Carlotta!'

Everyone, even those who had voted for Janet, cheered sportingly, and Janet was the first to shake Carlotta's hand, saying, 'The best girl won! Well done yet again!' Inwardly, though, she couldn't help but feel disappointed and a little resentful. This was the second time today she had lost out to Carlotta!

Quite unaware of the girl's feelings, Carlotta said sincerely, 'I don't know about being the best girl, but it certainly seems to be my lucky day.'

And it wasn't over yet! As the meeting broke up, Libby came across and said, 'Carlotta! I've asked Mum if you can come to tea with us on Saturday. If you come over early in the afternoon, we can get some riding in first. Do say you'll come!'

'Oh, yes!' exclaimed Carlotta, her dark eyes sparkling with anticipation. 'I'll have to get permission from Miss Adams, but I shouldn't think she'll say no. Thanks, Libby! It will be fun!'

'You can bet it will!' agreed Libby with a grin. 'I must say, I'm looking forward to having a friend who appreciates the important things in life – namely horses! I'm terribly fond of Fern, but we don't have much in common and her conversation bores me stiff most of the time.'

Carlotta felt a happy glow spreading through her. The girl was extremely popular with all of her form, but she had never had a special friend of her own. Carlotta hadn't minded, and had certainly never felt lonely at St Clare's but there was something very warming about the thought of having someone to confide in.

Alison, meanwhile, wasn't feeling quite so happy with her two new friendships. Rachel and Fern really disliked one another intensely and Alison didn't like being caught in the middle at all. She managed a few words alone with Fern, before the day girls went home, and said pleadingly, 'I do wish that you and Rachel would try to make friends. I like both of you so much and it makes things terribly difficult when you don't get on with one another.'

'Well, Alison, I can't understand what you see in Rachel, to be honest,' said Fern in her high, pretty voice. 'But as it's so important to you, I really will make an effort to be nice to her.' She smiled her sweetest smile, which a delighted Alison returned with one of her own.

Hilary, who happened to walk by just then, said to Pat later that she felt quite ill at such a display of sickly-sweetness.

But Alison was content, and made up her mind to speak to Rachel later. Perhaps they could be a threesome after all.

5

Settling down

As the first week went by, the three new girls settled down at St Clare's in their different ways. Rachel proved to be extremely clever at her lessons, especially English, but very often she seemed to go off into some sort of daydream – not a very happy one, to judge from her sombre expression. Her lapses in concentration sorely tried the mistresses' patience. Mam'zelle hardly knew what to make of her and was torn between delight and exasperation. Delight because Rachel's grasp of French grammar and her written work were exceptionally good. Exasperation because her accent was dreadful. The girls found this rather puzzling. As Doris, who could copy Mam'zelle's voice to perfection, said, 'I should have thought that an actress would be able to imitate any accent she chose.'

'Perhaps she isn't as good an actress as she makes out,' Fern had suggested with a touch of malice. She had kept her word to Alison and tried to be more pleasant to Rachel. But as Alison wasn't present when this conversation took place, she had felt quite safe getting a small dig in at Rachel.

Fern herself, thanks to her prettiness and charming manner, had swiftly become one of Mam'zelle's favourites, although her French was not at all good. In fact, Fern wasn't very good at any of her lessons. Miss Adams's sarcastic remarks went right over her pretty head and made no impression on her at all. She was very like Alison in her dislike of any form of sport, detesting anything that made her get hot and untidy.

Her cousin Libby, however, adored swimming and had a lovely, natural style at tennis. Jennifer Mills, the new games captain, called her over after watching her practise one day and said, 'Well done, kid! Carry on like this and you could well be in a few matches this term.'

Libby couldn't help flushing with pride at the bigger girl's words, but she said frankly, 'Thanks, Jenny, but I'm afraid all my spare time is spent with the horses, so I can't put in as much practice at tennis as I would like. I mean to make a career out of show-jumping, you see, so I really must devote as much time as I can to my riding.'

Jennifer, a keen horsewoman herself, understood at once and said, 'That's a pity, because you could have done well for St Clare's. Oh, well, Libby, if you ever change your mind and decide to concentrate on tennis instead of riding, let me know!'

Libby's attitude extended to the classroom as well. She was bright and could do well at most subjects – when she bothered to make the effort! As Janet said, 'Libby will never be really whole-hearted about anything other than her horses. I'm not sure whether that's a good thing or a bad one. Still, she's ever so nice and good fun.'

The whole form agreed that Libby was a livewire,

as they put it, and the girl soon became a firm favourite with everyone.

One lunch-time the third formers had found them-selves a sunny spot on one of St Clare's fine lawns and were enjoying the glorious weather.

'Mm, I could lie here all day,' sighed Hilary con-tentedly, stretching at full length on the grass. 'This hot weather always makes me feel so lazy.'

'Yes, it's lovely when we're outside,' agreed Bobby. 'But I just can't bear being cooped up indoors when the sun is shining. Then it has the opposite effect and makes me feel bored and restless – especially during maths and French *dictée*!'

Doris chuckled, knowing that when Bobby felt restless, it usually meant the class was in for some fun. 'Does this mean you're going to play a trick?' she asked hopefully.

'Doris! Nothing was further from my mind!' protested Bobby, making her eyes wide and innocent. 'Though, now that you mention it, there's nothing quite like a really good trick for letting off a bit of steam.'

Libby raised herself up on one elbow, an excited sparkle in her eyes. 'Who will you play it on?' she asked eagerly. 'Not Miss Adams, surely? She's far too sharp.'

'No, my dear Libby,' said Janet with a grin. 'Definitely not Miss Adams. There's really only one choice of victim when it comes to playing a trick – and that's Mam'zelle. Hey, Bobby, I wonder how many times you and I have caught her out over the years?'

'Dozens, I should think,' laughed Hilary. 'Remember

that trick you played, Bobby, when you made Mam'zelle's plate jump up and down? I thought my sides would split with laughing.'

'And that time back in the first form, Janet, when you filled her spectacle case with insects,' joined in Alison. 'Poor old Mam'zelle thought she was seeing things!'

'That one wasn't nearly so funny,' remembered Janet, pulling a wry face. 'I did it to get back at Mam'zelle for being so bad tempered that term, and it turned out that she was really ill. I felt so dreadful about it afterwards that it nearly cured me of playing tricks for good! Thank Heavens there was no harm done.'

'I just adore jokes and tricks, though I'm not very good at thinking them out,' said Libby. 'Oh, Bobby! Janet! *Do* play one on Mam'zelle! I'd just love to see her face.'

'It would be good fun,' said Bobby, her merry eyes crinkling mischievously. 'How about it, Janet?'

Janet, thinking that they would have a most appreciative audience in Libby, agreed readily. 'Though it's going to take us a little time to come up with an idea and plan it all out. I'm due a letter from my brother soon. Perhaps he'll have some ideas.'

'Janet's brother comes up with the most ingenious tricks,' explained Hilary to Libby. 'And he always passes them on to her. Which is wonderful for us, but not so good for Mam'zelle!'

'Poor Mam'zelle!' put in Fern with a pout. 'I think it's a shame to play jokes on her. She's such a decent sort!'

Libby pulled a face at her cousin. 'You only say that

because she believed that feeble excuse you made this morning about one of the horses eating your French prep! Anyway, it's only a bit of fun.'

'And dear old Mam'zelle always takes it in good part,' laughed Doris fondly.

But after Fern and Alison had moved away to join Rachel, who had just come outside, Doris said, 'Libby! That cousin of yours won't sneak to Mam'zelle, will she? That would really ruin everything.'

'Oh, Fern's all right,' Libby assured her airily. 'She can be a bit of an idiot at times, but she wouldn't tell tales.'

'Ah, Fern might not, but can we be so sure about our illustrious head girl?' said Janet slyly, nudging Bobby and nodding towards Carlotta, who was lying with her hands behind her head, half asleep.

'Hm?' The girl gave a yawn and stretched. 'What are you talking about?'

'We were just talking about playing a trick on Mam'zelle,' explained Bobby patiently. 'Fern doesn't approve – and Janet seems to think that as you're head of the form, you might not either.'

Carlotta sat bolt upright at this, saying with mock indignation, 'Does she indeed? Well, Janet, for your information, if I was head girl of the whole school I should still say go ahead and play your trick on Mam'zelle.'

Everyone laughed at this and Doris cried out, 'Good for you, Carlotta! We might have known that you wouldn't go all prim and proper on us!'

Carlotta laughed too, but she cast a sharp glance in

Janet's direction. The girl had made one or two pointed comments about her in the past couple of days and, although they had been laughed off, Carlotta couldn't rid herself of the idea that Janet was annoyed with her for some reason. Was it because she had been chosen to direct the play, perhaps? That might be part of it, but Carlotta had a strange feeling that it went deeper than that. It was all very odd, because Janet was normally every bit as frank and forthright as Carlotta herself, and would blow up if anyone upset her. Ruefully, Carlotta wished that she would blow up at her! At least it would clear the air between them, and anything would be better than this veiled hostility which wasn't Janet's style at all. Then, the next minute, Janet was her usual friendly self, punching Carlotta playfully on the arm as she reminded the girl of a trick the two of them had played on the sixth form last term. And, as Carlotta laughed with her, she began to wonder if she wasn't imagining things, and if Janet's change in attitude wasn't all in her own mind. It really was most perplexing and extremely annoying!

Equally annoying, as far as Alison was concerned, was the strained friendship between Fern and Rachel. Alison had spoken to Rachel the other night too, telling her that Fern had agreed to make an effort, and asking her to do the same.

'Well, I'll be pleasant for as long as she is,' had been Rachel's not very encouraging response. 'But *how* I dislike her! Nothing but a little feather-head, without a single sensible thought between her ears.'

Alison had bitten her lip at this and said, rather soberly, 'If only you knew how often the others have said exactly the same thing about me! And it's true. I know that I'm a bit of a dunce, and not exactly a deep thinker.' She frowned suddenly. 'But if Fern and I are so alike, how is it that you like me, but not her?'

Rachel clapped Alison on the shoulder, rather touched by her friend's little speech. 'You're only alike on the surface,' she said. 'And as for not being deep – well, at least you *have* something under *your* surface. You're warm, kind, sincere, loyal . . . everything that Fern isn't!'

'Oh!' exclaimed Alison, torn between pleasure at this glowing tribute and a wish to defend Fern. 'Well, thank you, Rachel. I'm glad that you feel like that about me. But I've always found Fern to be very warm and friendly.'

Rachel was shrewd and, unlike Alison, able to see beyond a pretty face. She had summed Fern up at a glance, had seen the spoilt, calculating girl behind the charming smile. But it was of no use to expect Alison to see Fern the same way. She would never believe ill of anyone she had taken a liking to unless she saw it with her own eyes. So Rachel summoned up a smile and said, 'Perhaps I'm being a bit hard on Fern and she'll turn out to be quite decent once I get to know her. Anyway, I'm willing to meet her half-way.'

Rachel was thinking of this conversation now as she stepped out into the bright sunshine and saw Fern and Alison laughing with a group of third formers. Alison smiled and got to her feet when she saw her, Fern

36

following suit. But Fern's smile, Rachel noticed, didn't quite reach her eyes.

'Hi!' said Alison. 'What have you been up to? Fern and I have been out here for ages.'

'Oh, I thought I had better tidy my corner of the dormitory before Matron spotted it,' answered Rachel.

'Tidying up inside on a glorious day like this!' said Fern with a shudder. 'How dull! Still, I dare say life at St Clare's must seem pretty dull to you altogether.'

'What do you mean by that?' asked Rachel sharply.

Fern raised her finely arched brows at the girl's tone and said, 'Why, only that a school like this must seem terribly boring when you're used to mixing with theatrical types all the time.'

'Oh, I see!' Rachel seemed to relax a little. 'Well, Fern, theatrical types can be just as tiresome and boring as anyone else when you're with them every day.'

'I suppose so,' said Fern with her high little laugh. 'Which drama school did you go to, by the way?'

'The De Winter Academy,' answered Rachel. 'It's a very good one.'

'What a coincidence!' exclaimed Fern, clapping her hands together. 'A friend of mine from prep school goes there. Sara Jameson! We still keep in touch. Do you know her?'

'Yes.' Rachel had turned suddenly pale, the word forced out through stiff lips, while Fern and Alison stared at her curiously. 'Yes, I know Sara. Er . . . excuse me, would you? I've just remembered something I have to do.'

With that, Rachel sped away towards the school, leaving Alison and Fern to stare after her in surprise.

'Well, how peculiar!' exclaimed Alison, astonished. 'Did you see how white and upset she looked?'

Fern nodded while her mind worked rapidly. Rachel was obviously badly shaken by the fact that she, Fern, knew one of her fellow drama students. It was beginning to look as though the girl had something to hide. The question was, what? Fern made up her mind to find out. It was time, she thought, grinning slyly to herself, that she wrote to Sara Jameson.

6

A wonderful day

The first week of term really flew by and at last it was Saturday, when the girls were free to do as they pleased.

Many of them went into town to spend their pocket-money, meet in the coffee shop, or see a film. Others took advantage of the fine weather to swim, play tennis or just sunbathe. Carlotta was particularly excited today, for she was to spend the afternoon at Libby's. How she looked forward to meeting her friend's family – and the horses, of course!

She arrived at the Oaks early and, instead of going straight to the house and knocking on the door, she went across to the paddock. Leaning on the gate she watched critically as a tall, thin boy, who looked very like Libby, rode a huge black horse around. The horse was obviously a wild, high-spirited creature, rearing and bucking violently in an effort to throw its rider. But the boy was a fine horseman, noted Carlotta with approval, and stayed firmly in the saddle. Suddenly he spotted Carlotta and turned the horse towards the gate.

'Hallo, there!' called out Carlotta in her friendly manner. 'You must be Will! I'm Carlotta Brown.'

To the girl's dismay, her bright smile was met with a

scowl and Will replied with a bored air, 'I know. Libby has had to pop into town with Mum and Fern, but she won't be long. She asked me to look after you until she gets back.' A task that he evidently wasn't looking forward to, realized Carlotta, feeling her temper beginning to rise.

The boy looked her up and down disdainfully, then ordered curtly, 'Wait here. I'll see if we've got a horse suitable for you.'

While Will went off towards the stables, Carlotta reached up to pat the neck of the black horse. The animal tossed its head and reared away.

'Come on, boy,' she crooned softly. 'Come to Carlotta.'

The horse became still suddenly, then moved slowly forward, until he was directly in front of her. This time when she reached up to stroke him, the animal didn't break away, laying his big head on her shoulder.

'Hey! What on earth do you think you're doing?' The angry shout, coming from behind her, made Carlotta spin round sharply. She came face to face with an absolutely furious Will. 'Don't you realize he could have bitten you?' said the boy angrily.

'Of course he won't bite me!' snapped Carlotta, getting more annoyed by the second at his manner.

'That's all you know! Rocky isn't fully broken in yet and he has a vicious temper. *You* certainly wouldn't be able to handle him. My sister is the only girl I know who can ride a horse properly, and even she can't control Rocky.'

With an effort, Carlotta swallowed a cutting retort. She wasn't going to lose her temper. Instead, she was going to teach Libby's stuck-up brother a lesson!

'I'm sorry,' she said meekly, moving away from Rocky. 'Is this the horse I'm to ride?' Carlotta nodded towards the plump, docile little mare that Will was leading and the boy said shortly, 'Yes. Have you ridden before?'

'Just a little,' she answered diffidently.

'Well, you shouldn't have any trouble handling old Maisie here,' said Will with a patronizing air that made Carlotta's hackles rise. 'Do you think you can manage to mount by yourself?'

'Oh, I'm quite sure that I can't,' said Carlotta, opening her dark eyes wide in pretend dismay. 'Don't you have something that I could stand on?'

Heaving a sigh of irritation, Will dropped Maisie's reins and turned back towards the stables to get a mounting-block. Carlotta pulled a face at his departing back, then sped across to the gate, climbing nimbly over it and into Rocky's paddock. By the time Will returned, she was on the horse's back.

'Get down from there right now, you idiot!' he cried, dropping the block and springing towards the gate. 'You'll break your neck!'

'Pah!' was Carlotta's only reply, delivered with a toss of her dark head, before she made a soft clicking sound and Rocky took off as though he had winged hooves! Indeed, the horse moved so swiftly that, for a moment, Will really feared that he had bolted with Carlotta and decided that he had better ride to her rescue. Then he noticed her relaxed, light touch on the reins and the natural grace of her posture, and realized that she didn't need rescuing at all. Rocky hadn't bolted with Carlotta. *She* had bolted with *him* and, to Will's astonishment, was very much in charge of the situation! Just then Will's mother came into the stableyard, along with Libby and Fern.

'Will!' cried out Mrs Francis in alarm. 'What are you thinking putting that poor girl up on Rocky? Ride after them this instant!'

'Don't worry about Carlotta, Mum!' laughed Libby. 'She used to ride in a circus. Wow, just look at her go!'

'A circus?' repeated Will with a groan of dismay. 'Oh, no! Libby, why on earth didn't you tell me that? Now I've just made a complete idiot of myself!'

'Well, there's nothing new in that,' giggled Libby. 'You're always making an idiot of yourself. Hey, Carlotta! Come and meet my mum.'

Carlotta reined in the horse and dismounted, coming through the gate.

'So you're Carlotta,' said Mrs Francis with a friendly smile. 'Libby's been singing your praises all week, so it's nice to meet you at last. We'll be seeing a lot of you here, I hope?'

'If you'll have me,' said Carlotta with a grin, liking her friend's mother at once.

'The children's friends are always welcome here,' Mrs Francis said. 'Now, I dare say you could all do with a cold drink, so I'll put a bottle of lemonade out on the kitchen table. Come and get it when you're ready.'

She went into the house, leaving the four young

people together. Libby said wickedly, 'I don't need to introduce you to my big ape of a brother. Obviously you've already met.'

'Big ape is right,' said Will with a rueful smile. 'Carlotta, I really am sorry for speaking to you the way I did.'

Never one to bear a grudge, Carlotta found herself smiling back, liking the boy's frankness. 'Apology accepted. And I'm afraid I ought to say sorry to poor Maisie here,' said Carlotta, going across to the placid mare and stroking her nose. 'I brushed you aside most rudely, didn't I, sweetheart?'

'Will! You surely *didn't* try to get Carlotta up on dear old Maisie?' gasped Libby, torn between amusement and dismay. 'I'm surprised that she's speaking to you at all!'

Fern, who had been hovering uncertainly on the edge of the group, looking a little bored, piped up, 'Will, we've had a brilliant time in town! Just wait until you see the new dress that Aunt Polly bought me!'

Will glanced briefly at his cousin and nodded vaguely, before saying, 'Libby, let's go and get some of that lemonade, then we can introduce Carlotta to the rest of the horses.'

'Good idea,' said Libby. 'Come on, Carlotta!'

'Oh, don't say you're going to spend *all* afternoon with the horses,' wailed Fern with her now familiar pout. 'Will, you *promised* that you'd help me with my maths prep today!'

'Later,' said Will, with an impatient wave of his hand. 'Carlotta, you must teach Libby and me some of your circus tricks! Can you ride bareback? I can't wait to tell the guys at school all about you!'

Carlotta grinned, but her shrewd eyes rested on Fern, who was looking extremely unhappy at the way her cousin had brushed her aside. Carlotta didn't much like the girl, but in that moment she felt a little sorry for her. She gave Fern a warm smile, and was taken aback to receive a ferocious scowl in return. Then Fern turned away and stalked off into the house.

Yet, despite Fern's sulks, it was a most enjoyable day. An afternoon spent riding and grooming the horses, then a delicious picnic tea on the lawn. Libby and Will's parents joined them and it was a very happy meal, Mr Francis keeping everyone in stitches with his jokes.

After tea Mrs Francis offered to drive Carlotta back to school, but Will said, 'I've a better idea! Let's go on horseback instead! Carlotta can ride Silver, and I'll lead him back once we've dropped her off at St Clare's.'

'That's not fair!' protested Fern. 'I won't be able to come with you.'

'Well, it's your own fault if you won't learn to ride,' said Will, with a touch of scorn. 'You're such a baby, squealing and running away every time one of the horses so much as whinnies at you!'

For a moment Carlotta thought that Fern was going to burst into tears, then Mrs Francis said sternly, 'That was very unkind, Will! Fern can't help it if she's not a "horsey" person.'

'Sorry,' mumbled Will, turning a little red.

'Why don't we walk?' suggested Carlotta. 'It won't take us very long, and then Fern can come with us.' This was really very generous of Carlotta, for she would have much preferred to go on horseback. But she realized how left out Fern must feel, living with her horse-mad cousins. The girl didn't seem very grateful, though, giving Carlotta a sour glance that made her pretty face look quite ugly for a moment. She was unusually silent on the walk to St Clare's, too, but none of the others seemed to notice, chattering happily among themselves. Carlotta felt quite flat once they reached the school gates and Libby said, 'See you on Monday, Carlotta.'

'Thanks for a lovely day,' answered Carlotta. 'Goodbye. Goodbye, Fern.'

'Come again soon, won't you?' said Will, adding with a cheeky grin, 'You're not a bad sort – for a girl!'

'And I suppose you're quite decent – for a boy!' Carlotta retorted wickedly.

What a lovely day it had been, thought the girl happily, as she went in search of the third formers. She couldn't wait to tell them all about it. And how marvellous that she had made another friend in Will. Carlotta didn't realize that she had also made an enemy in Fern, for the girl had an extremely jealous nature. A spoilt only child, Fern was used to having the undivided attention of her doting parents. When anyone she liked showed the slightest interest in anyone other than herself, she was quite unable to bear it.

Fern brooded over Carlotta on the way home. Will had treated the girl almost like a sister, she thought jealously, while he hardly paid any attention to her at all. As for

Uncle Tom, he never laughed and joked with her as he had with Carlotta. Even Aunt Polly had made a fuss of her, as if Carlotta was one of the family. It just wasn't fair! First there was that awful Rachel, trying to take Alison away from her, and now that horrible little Carlotta seemed to want to take her place with the family. Well, she would just have to do something about both of them!

An announcement - and a plan

There was great excitement in the third form common-room, for Carlotta had called a meeting to announce which script had been chosen for the end-of-term play. Several of the girls had begun writing scripts, but had soon discovered that it wasn't as easy as they had thought. Pat and Isabel were among those who had fallen by the wayside, their effort – after much sighing, soul-searching and crossing out – finding its way into the wastepaper bin.

'I think we have to face the fact that we just don't have the talent to write a play,' Pat had remarked ruefully.

'After that lame effort, I'm not sure that we have the talent to write a nursery rhyme!' Isabel had said with a sigh. 'Let's just hope the others have done better, or we shan't have a play at all.'

In the end, three scripts were submitted, and Miss Adams and Carlotta read them all carefully. In spite of the fact that the writers hadn't given their names, Carlotta recognized Doris's work at once. Her wonderful sense of humour shone through every line, and Carlotta chuckled as she read it.

The second script was a very dramatic one, and certainly a praiseworthy effort. But the third, agreed

Carlotta and Miss Adams, was outstanding. 'Whoever wrote this has a very bright future ahead of her!' exclaimed Miss Adams. 'It really is excellent.'

'Yes, and it has a few humorous touches, as well as some dramatic moments, so it ought to please everyone,' said Carlotta, delighted.

She looked at the cover and read out the title of the play. '"Lady Dorinda's Diamonds." I wonder if this is Hilary's work? If so, she's been hiding her light under a bushel.'

But the mystery writer wasn't Hilary. In fact, it was the last person Carlotta expected!

She entered the common-room with the script under her arm and smiled round at the waiting girls. 'First of all, I'd like to thank the three of you who handed in plays,' she said, sitting down. 'They were all very good and you must have worked very hard indeed. It's a pity that we could only choose one, but here it is – "Lady Dorinda's Diamonds". I'm going to read out the first act, then we'll get the writer to come forward, and give her a round of applause!'

The girls listened attentively as Carlotta began to read, swiftly becoming enthralled as the story unfolded.

'Isn't it marvellous?' whispered Isabel to Pat.

'I'll say! Our feeble effort wouldn't have stood a chance!'

At last Carlotta came to the end of the first act and looked round expectantly, waiting for the girls' reaction. And what a reaction! There was silence for a moment, then the whole room erupted, the third formers cheering, clapping and whistling, so that Mam'zelle, marking books in the room below, thought that the ceiling was about to come down!

'Absolutely brilliant!'

'Bravo!'

'This is really going to make the parents sit up and take notice!'

'Writer! Writer!' called someone, and all the girls took up the cry, until Carlotta, raising her voice above the others, shouted, 'Yes, stand up, whoever you are!'

She glanced towards Hilary as she spoke, half expecting her to come forward. But a movement came from the other side of the room and a slim figure got to her feet. Rachel! The girls were stunned into silence for a moment. Fancy *Rachel*, who seemed to think herself a cut above the third formers, bothering to write a play for them – and such a good play, too! The girl at once went up in everyone's estimation, blushing and looking rather shy as the cheering started again, several girls reaching out to clap her on the back. Only Fern remained silent and tight lipped, resenting the attention the girl was receiving, especially when Alison called out, 'Well done, Rachel!'

'Thank you,' said Rachel hesitantly, taking her place beside Carlotta. 'I'm so glad that you like it.'

'I'll say we do!' exclaimed Carlotta, still feeling surprised that Rachel had turned out to be the anonymous writer. 'And now we can get down to the business of giving out parts and rehearsing. I'll arrange to have some copies of the script printed so that everyone can read through it properly, and we'll hold auditions in the hall next Sunday at two o'clock sharp.'

A babble of excited chatter broke out and Fern, completely forgetting that she was supposed to be making an effort to like Rachel, said spitefully to Alison, 'This is going to make Rachel even more swollen headed and unbearable. I think she's a sly creature, too. Fancy writing a play in secret and not even letting on to you, her best friend, about it.'

'Oh, she did tell me,' said Alison. 'But I promised to keep it to myself. Rachel didn't want anyone else to know in case her script was no good and she decided not to submit it.'

'Well, you *are* changing for the better, Alison,' exclaimed Janet, overhearing this. 'Not so long ago, telling you a secret was the surest way of spreading it round the whole school!'

Alison pulled a face at Janet, who laughed. Alison really was changing! A few terms ago, a teasing remark like that would have made her burst into tears. Fern, however, was not amused, hating the thought of Alison sharing a secret with Rachel and not letting her in on it. Worse still, she couldn't even punish Alison by sulking, for that would only drive her closer to Rachel. Fern really felt that life was very unfair at that moment!

As the girls began to drift away, Carlotta called out to Janet and Rachel, 'I wondered if you two would be decent enough to help me out with the auditions on Sunday? It's going to be quite a task, fitting the right part to the right person. Janet, you're always clear headed, so you ought to be a big help. And Rachel, you've had some experience at this kind of thing, so you should know how to make everything run smoothly.'

'I'd love to help,' said Janet at once, forgetting for the moment that she was still feeling a little sore with Carlotta.

'So would I,' agreed Rachel, who felt happier now than she had done in a long time. And what a difference it made, thought Carlotta, thinking how pretty and pleasant the girl looked, with her flushed cheeks and sparkling eyes.

'Great!' she said, pleased. 'It should be good fun.'

The girls were in for some fun before the auditions, too, thanks to Bobby and Janet.

The following day, Janet received a small package from her brother, and she and Bobby opened it together in the dormitory.

'Well, this doesn't look very thrilling!' said Bobby, disappointed, as she picked up what looked like a reel of thread. 'I don't see how we can trick Mam'zelle with this.'

Janet, who had been reading the letter that had come with the package, chuckled and said, 'You will! Here, read this.'

Bobby took the letter, and soon a grin spread across her mischievous face. 'Brilliant!' she cried. 'Janet, this could be our best trick yet.'

'And I think I know how to improve on it,' said Janet, opening her locker and rummaging around in it. 'Ah, here we are!' She produced a small tin with holes in the top, and Bobby said curiously, 'Whatever is that?'

'It's called a noise-box,' Janet told her. 'I've had it for ages, but haven't been able to find a use for it. I think I've found one now, though. Just listen.'

Janet turned the little tin upside down and it emitted a long, mournful wail.

'Marvellous!' breathed Bobby. 'Janet, let's play it on Friday, when Mam'zelle means to read us that French book!'

'The ghost story, you mean?' said Janet with a wicked grin. 'This just gets better and better, Bobby! Now, let's go and tell the others.'

At break that morning a group of third formers, led by Bobby and Janet, entered their classroom.

'Come on, Janet,' said Pat impatiently. 'We're just dying to see what you've got planned.'

'All right. Isabel, stand by the door will you, in case one of the mistresses comes along,' said Janet, producing the thread and the noise-box from her pocket.

'Why, it looks just like a reel of ordinary sewing cotton,' said Hilary.

'Ah, this is no ordinary cotton,' Janet said. 'Watch this!' Deftly she tied one end to the cord hanging from the blind at the window, then stepped back. 'See? The thread is almost invisible.'

'I see,' said Doris, 'Or rather, I *don't* see! Now what?'

In answer, Janet tugged on the invisible thread and the blind came whooshing down. 'We can make all sorts of things move simply by attaching a length of thread and pulling on it,' explained Bobby. 'We'll have poor old Mam'zelle believing that the room is haunted. And this will help.' She turned over the noise-box and it gave its spine-chilling wail, making Libby shiver.

'Ooh, that sounds really eerie!' she cried. 'My goodness, what a wonderful trick this is going to be!'

'We'll have to make sure that all the lengths of thread are in place before Mam'zelle comes in,' said Janet, who liked everything to be just perfect when she was planning a trick. 'A few of us will have to come in at break-time on Friday and see to that. And it won't be at all difficult to get Mam'zelle on to the subject of ghosts, seeing as we shall be reading that spooky French story.'

'I can't wait!' cried Doris excitedly. 'Roll on Friday!'

A ghostly trick

The next two days seemed to crawl by, but at last it was Friday and time for the third form's French lesson.

Bobby, Janet and the twins sneaked into the classroom at break-time, cutting off long lengths of the magic thread and tying them to cupboard handles, empty chairs, the ceiling light – anything, in fact, that could be easily moved.

'Mam'zelle's always such a wonderful person to play a trick on,' chuckled Isabel in gleeful anticipation. 'She *always* falls for it, and never ever suspects that we might have anything to do with the mysterious things that are going on.'

'Well, there will be some very mysterious happenings in here today, all right,' said Pat with a grin. 'I just hope that no one gives the game away by laughing too much.'

Mam'zelle was in good humour when she entered the classroom. The morning post had brought her a long and chatty letter from one of her adored nieces, and she had just enjoyed a most peaceful and rewarding lesson with the sixth form, who were all good, hard-working girls.

Little guessing that her peace was about to be rudely shattered, she beamed round at the third formers, saying happily, 'Sit, *mes filles*. Now, today we will continue to read the ghost story which we started last week. Hilary, begin.'

'Oh, Mam'zelle, must we?' pleaded Hilary, making her eyes wide and scared. 'It really gives me the creeps.'

'Ah, it is just a story, *mon enfant*,' Mam'zelle assured her kindly. 'There are no such things as ghosts.'

'Well, I wouldn't be too sure about that, Mam'zelle,' put in Doris darkly. 'I got a book from the library the other day, which said that St Clare's itself is supposed to be haunted.'

Alison gave a realistic shudder and Doris continued, 'By a faceless monk, who roams the corridors and class-rooms, wailing and . . .'

'Enough!' broke in Mam'zelle, losing some of her good humour. 'There are no monks at St Clare's, faceless or otherwise. The good Miss Theobald would never permit it!'

Mirabel gave a giggle, which she hastily turned into a cough, and Mam'zelle repeated firmly, 'There are no such things as ghosts, I tell you. Hilary, please read.'

Hilary began, and Janet waited until she was half-way down the page before operating the little noise-box which was in her pocket.

Libby squealed. 'Mam'zelle! What was that?'

The French mistress looked most astonished for a moment then, recovering herself, said briskly, 'It must have been the school cat, outside the window. Gladys, you take over the story, please.'

It was as Gladys reached a very tense, frightening part of the tale that Bobby tugged the end of the thread nearest her and the blind came down with a terrific clatter.

'*Tiens*!' exclaimed Mam'zelle, putting a hand to her heart. 'What a startle that gave me!'

'You mean a start, Mam'zelle,' giggled Isabel. 'What on earth could have caused that?'

'If you ask me, it wasn't anything on earth,' said Doris gravely. 'I think it was the ghost of . . .'

'Doris! One more word about faceless monks, and I send you outside!' threatened Mam'zelle, her glasses slipping down her nose as they were prone to do in moments of emotion. 'See, the window is open! It must have been the wind.' She conveniently overlooked the fact that it was a perfectly calm day without so much as a breeze, giving the girls a stern look that dared them to contradict her. 'Gladys,' she ordered firmly. 'Continue!'

Pat waited until Gladys made a mistake in her reading before pulling her thread. Then the door of the cupboard flew violently open, and Pat gave a well-feigned jump. 'Mam'zelle, I don't like this at all!' she cried, looking frightened. 'There seems to be something awfully strange going on in here today.'

Mam'zelle was beginning to look a little alarmed now, but said staunchly, 'Doors do not open themselves. One of you girls at the back must have pulled it open!'

'But, Mam'zelle, none of us is close enough,' pointed out Janet. 'And you can see for yourself that no one has moved from their seats.'

As she finished speaking, Janet set off the noise-box again, and poor Mam'zelle stood frozen to the spot in terror.

Doris, unable to control herself any longer, gave a snort of laughter, which set off Libby and Carlotta, both of whom hid behind their books to disguise their giggles. Then Janet caught the eyes of the girls around her and gave a little nod. Everything seemed to happen at once after that. The light above the French mistress's head began to swing back and forth. An empty chair beside Rachel suddenly toppled over backwards and the blackboard rubber flew from its ledge. And all the while a mournful wailing went on in the background. Mam'zelle gave a shriek and staggered back, almost overbalancing.

'Ah, *mon dieu, mon dieu*!' she cried. 'It is indeed true! The classroom is haunted.'

This was too much for the girls, who began to laugh helplessly. Isabel almost fell off her chair, while Hilary held her sides. Gladys and Mirabel clung to one another as tears of mirth poured down their cheeks.

Mam'zelle took one look at the chaos in the classroom and fled to find help. The girls gave full rein to their laughter.

'A monk with no face!' gasped Carlotta.

'Ah, *mon dieu, mon dieu*!' cried Doris, in a fine imitation of Mam'zelle's voice. 'Oh, I shall be sick if I laugh any more!'

Even Fern, who had been against the trick at the beginning, was doubled up with laughter, while Rachel was quite convulsed.

'Listen,' said Pat, when she could control her laughter enough to speak. 'Where do you suppose Mam'zelle went?'

'I hope she hasn't gone to Miss Theobald,' said Hilary. 'Although even if we get into a row, I shall still say it was worth it. Did you see her face when the light began to swing to and fro?'

That set them all off again and in a few minutes the whole class was helpless.

Mam'zelle, meanwhile, *had* gone to the head, quite convinced that the third-form classroom was inhabited by a ghost. The head looked up, startled, when the French mistress burst into her room without knocking, and was quite alarmed by her pallor.

'Why, Mam'zelle, you're trembling!' she cried. 'Whatever is the matter?'

'Ah, Miss Theobald, you would not believe what has happened in the third-form classroom,' groaned Mam'zelle, sinking on to a chair. 'It is haunted. There is a ghost and it is quite invisible!'

Miss Theobald, knowing Mam'zelle's excitable ways, hid a smile and said calmly, 'Perhaps you had better tell me exactly what happened.'

'It started with a truly terrible wailing noise, like a soul in torment. Then books and furniture began to fly about the room of their own accord. The poor girls are in a state of terror.'

'Really?' said the head drily. 'Bobby and Janet are in the third form, aren't they, Mam'zelle?'

Mam'zelle's glasses began to slip down her nose once more as she realized what Miss Theobald was suggesting. 'It is not a trick!' she declared firmly. 'It is quite impossible that the dear girls could have made such things happen.'

The head felt that where Bobby and Janet were concerned, nothing was impossible! Getting to her feet, she said briskly, 'Well, Mam'zelle, let's go and investigate.'

The third formers had calmed down a little by the time Mam'zelle returned, and they sobered up completely when Miss Theobald entered behind her. A deathly hush fell over the room as the girls hastily stood up.

'See, Miss Theobald!' exclaimed Mam'zelle. 'There is the chair which fell over, and see how the blackboard rubber flew through the air!'

Bobby, who had more daring than any girl in the class, still had in her hand the thread which was attached to the light, and couldn't resist a wicked impulse to give it another tug.

Mam'zelle screamed and clutched at Miss Theobald. 'Ah, the spirit is still here!' she cried.

The head looked from the swinging light to Bobby, who was wearing a most innocent expression. This alone was enough to confirm Miss Theobald's suspicions and she went across to the girl, saying coldly, 'Roberta, what is that in your hand?'

Bobby opened her hand which, at first glance, appeared empty. But Miss Theobald's eyes were sharp and, as she leant forward, she could see something against the girl's palm.

'Mam'zelle, I think Roberta can provide an explanation as to the strange goings on in here,' said the head. 'I will leave you to deal with the matter.' With that she left the room and Bobby waited for Mam'zelle's wrath to descend on her bent head.

'So!' cried the Frenchwoman. 'A trick! How was this abominable thing done?'

Bobby explained about the thread, while Janet removed the noise-box from her pocket, making it wail once more.

'I see,' said Mam'zelle, returning to her desk. The class waited with bated breath as she stared straight ahead of her, the sloe-black eyes solemn. All was silent for several moments. Then Mam'zelle began to chuckle. Softly at first, then more loudly, until she was positively roaring with laughter, her head thrown back and tears streaming down her cheeks. The girls began to grin too, liking Mam'zelle for being able to take a joke. They were relieved as well! If the French mistress could see the funny side, nothing too terrible would happen to them. But Mam'zelle wasn't letting them off scot-free.

'Ah, you bad girls!' she cried, with a twinkle in her eye. 'As a punishment, you will translate the first two chapters of the story we have been reading and have it ready for me by Monday!'

The third formers groaned inwardly, but no one dared protest out loud, for they knew that they had earned their punishment. Indeed, as Doris said later, 'If it had been any other mistress, we wouldn't have got off nearly so lightly! We can count ourselves lucky that Mam'zelle is such a sport.'

'Isn't she just,' chuckled Bobby. 'All the same, we had

better not play any more tricks on her for a bit. I don't think there's much chance of her being so lenient with us a second time.'

'No,' said Pat with a grin. 'Not even the *ghost* of a chance!'

Carlotta in hot water

On the day of the auditions, Carlotta spent the morning riding with Libby. She had become a regular visitor at the Oaks and was quite one of the family, as Libby put it.

Libby and Fern were in the stableyard when Carlotta arrived and called out, 'Hi, you two!'

'Carlotta. You here again?' said Fern pointedly. 'Really, you might as well move in here and become a day girl at St Clare's, just like Libby and me.'

'Fern!' cried her cousin, quite shocked at the girl's rudeness. 'How dare you! Carlotta is a guest here – a very welcome guest – and I won't have her spoken to like that!'

'Well, she's obviously a lot more welcome here than I am!' snapped Fern. 'Perhaps you'd like me to move out of my bedroom so that she can come here permanently!'

'Well!' exclaimed Carlotta, as Fern flounced off. 'What's got into her? I know I'm not exactly Fern's favourite person, but she's never attacked me directly like that before.'

'Oh, she's just jealous because you've made such a hit with Will and my parents,' said Libby, exasperated by her cousin. 'You know how soppy she is about Will, yet he doesn't see her as anything but a perfect pest. Then you come along and he starts treating you like another sister.'

'Poor Fern,' said Carlotta. 'No wonder she's got such a down on me.'

'Poor Fern nothing!' scoffed Libby. 'She's been spoilt and pampered all her life, thanks to my aunt and uncle. It will do her good to realize that she can't wind everyone round her little finger.'

'I suppose so,' laughed Carlotta. 'By the way, where *are* Will and your parents? It seems awfully quiet here today.'

'They're out visiting friends,' Libby explained. 'Fern and I were invited too, but it would have meant missing the auditions.'

'Are you going in for one of the leading parts?' asked Carlotta.

'Heavens, no! A walk-on part will suit me,' answered Libby. 'I don't want to have to spend all my spare time rehearsing when I could be out riding. I must say, I'm rather sorry that you're director. You won't be able to come over here nearly so often.'

'You're right!' said Carlotta in dismay. 'I hadn't thought of that! I almost wish that I'd let Janet have the job now. Oh, well, I'd better make the most of the time I have got, then. How about a race?'

The two girls spent a blissful hour riding, then went into the kitchen for a simple but scrumptious lunch of crusty bread, cheese and salad, followed by cold apple pie with cream.

Fern joined them, getting up from the table as soon as

she had finished eating and saying shortly, 'I'm going across to St Clare's now.'

'Why?' asked Libby in surprise. 'The auditions don't start for ages.'

'I know, but I'm going for the part of Lady Dorinda, and Alison has promised to read through it with me so that I'm word perfect.'

'Best of luck,' said Carlotta. 'Hey, Libby, we'd better keep an eye on the time. It will never do if I'm late for the auditions.'

'The stable clock keeps good time,' replied Libby. 'Come on, let's clear up quickly, then we can get back to the horses.'

Fern was thoughtful as she stepped out into the bright sunshine. Carlotta *would* be in hot water with the rest of the form if she turned up late this afternoon. The third took their responsibilities very seriously indeed and looked to Carlotta, as head girl, for a lead. Making a sudden decision, Fern ran to the stables, getting out a small stepladder and placing it beneath the stable clock. It was set above the doors and, even on the top step, she had to stand on tiptoe, stretching her arms high above her head to reach the hands. But she managed it, setting the clock back by a full hour. Smiling triumphantly to herself, she replaced the steps, then made her way out of the yard into the lane. Even if she didn't get the part of Lady Dorinda, Fern was really going to enjoy today's auditions!

'Where on earth has Carlotta got to?' said Pat impatiently,

looking at her watch. 'It's almost quarter past two and no sign of her!'

'It really is too bad of her when the rest of us have made the effort to turn up on time,' said Janet irritably. 'Hey, Fern, do you have any idea where she and Libby could have got to?'

'Oh, you know what Carlotta's like,' answered Fern with a laugh. 'Once she gets on horseback, nothing else seems to matter. I shouldn't be surprised if she's forgotten about the auditions altogether!'

'Well, I vote we start without her,' said Hilary. 'Otherwise we're just wasting everyone's time. If Carlotta doesn't like it, that's just too bad.'

'Right,' said Janet, taking charge. 'We'll cast the part of Lady Dorinda first, as she's the main character. Fern, you can go first, then Gladys.' She took a seat beside Rachel, and the two of them watched critically as Fern took centre stage. 'She certainly looks the part,' murmured Janet. 'But she couldn't act her way out of a paper bag!'

Rachel nodded agreement as Fern flung herself about the stage, almost shouting the lines and accompanying them with dramatic gestures. Several of the watching girls had to smother giggles at the terribly refined voice Fern put on, which was quite different from her own pleasant tone. At last, unable to bear any more, Janet stood up and called out, 'Thank you, Fern! I think we've seen enough. Gladys, your turn now.'

A small, almost insignificant figure, Gladys looked pale and nervous as she took the stage, and Rachel frowned.

This mousy little creature would never be able to play the beautiful, spirited Lady Dorinda convincingly! But Rachel was wrong. Gladys didn't just *play* Lady Dorinda, she became her, her speech and movements fluid and natural. When she had finished, the watching girls applauded and cheered loudly.

'Wow, what a talent!' exclaimed Rachel, absolutely thrilled. To hear Gladys speak the words she had written, and breathe life into the character she had created, had been strangely moving. Rachel had felt a lump form in her throat. She and Janet were in complete agreement – Gladys just *had* to play Lady Dorinda!

Tall, strapping Mirabel was given the part of her absent-minded husband, while Doris was just marvellous in a comic role as a bumbling policeman. 'She'll bring the house down,' said Rachel happily. 'Doris is every bit as gifted as Gladys, though in a completely different way.'

Janet nodded, surprised and pleased at the change in Rachel, and at how well the two of them worked together. She had been afraid that the girl, with her drama school training, might have been critical and hard to please, but she was extremely sincere and generous in her praise. Slightly to her shame, Janet was also delighted by the chance to show the others how smoothly she could make things run in Carlotta's absence. And, certainly, she made the auditions run like clockwork, so that by ten minutes to three all of the leading roles had been filled and there now remained only the minor parts to cast. This was when Carlotta and Libby turned up and the sight of them, laughing and chattering away to one another as they strolled into the hall, annoyed many of the girls intensely.

'Good of you to put in an appearance!' called out Janet, with sarcasm. 'I do hope that we haven't interrupted your horse riding.'

Hearing the edge to Janet's voice, and suddenly aware of the hard stares which many of the girls were giving her, Carlotta came to an abrupt halt in the middle of the floor. 'What's up?' she asked in surprise. 'Oh, don't say you've started without us! That was a bit mean!'

'Well, it's rather mean to turn up late!' cried Bobby indignantly. 'You surely didn't expect us to sit around doing nothing for the best part of an hour while we waited for you to grace us with your presence?'

'Bobby, whatever do you mean?' said Carlotta, completely bewildered by the girl's tone. 'It's only ten to two.'

'Actually, Carlotta, it's ten to *three*,' pointed out Pat drily.

'But that's impossible!' put in Libby with a frown. 'We left home at precisely twenty to two by the stable clock.'

'Well, your clock must be wrong,' said Isabel. 'Because you're almost an hour late.'

'Oh, no!' wailed Carlotta in dismay. 'Girls, I really am sorry!'

'It's my fault,' said Libby apologetically. 'I was quite certain that the clock was right.'

'Well, it can't be helped now,' said Hilary sensibly. 'I'm afraid we just had to carry on without you, though, and most of the parts have been filled.'

'I see.' Carlotta walked across to Janet and Rachel,

looking down at the notebook that lay between them. There was a neatly written list of all the characters and, beside each one, the name of the girl who was to play the part. 'Well, the two of you seem to have done an excellent job,' said Carlotta generously, trying to keep the disappointment from her voice. 'Would you like me to take over now?'

'That's hardly fair,' protested Mirabel. 'Janet and Rachel have done all the donkey work and now you want to push them aside.'

'I don't want to do anything of the kind!' retorted Carlotta, stung. 'I was late due to a simple mistake, I've apologized, and now I want to make up for it by pulling my weight. What's wrong with that?'

Fern, in the background, almost hugged herself with glee. Her mean little trick had gone better than expected, and no one had the slightest suspicion that she had put the clock back. And there would be plenty more tricks where that one came from!

'Let's calm down a little,' suggested the steady Hilary. 'Carlotta, why don't you let Rachel and Janet finish dishing out the parts, seeing as they've done such a marvellous job? And in the meantime you can set about working out a timetable for rehearsals.'

Carlotta gave Hilary a grateful smile. 'Good idea,' she said. 'I'll just find myself a sheet of paper and a quiet corner.'

So the situation was resolved and Carlotta's lapse was forgiven. But not all of the girls forgot about it. Fern thought about it often, rejoicing at the trouble she had caused and plotting further revenge, as she thought of it, against both Carlotta and Rachel. And the incident remained in Janet's mind too. Carlotta had shown that she was unreliable and she might well do so again. The girl had better watch her step!

10

A birthday party

Carlotta did watch her step, extremely conscious of the fact that she had blotted her copybook with the third form and anxious not to repeat the mistake. The first couple of rehearsals went smoothly, with everyone present on time and the cast enthusiastic. Everybody was looking forward to the end-of-term play enormously.

There were other things for the girls to look forward to as well. There was tennis and swimming, of course, which most of them loved. Then half-term was coming up shortly, and everyone was dying to see parents, brothers and sisters again. Best of all, there were several form birthdays coming up – and birthdays meant parties!

First was Libby's, and her parents threw a party at the Oaks one Saturday afternoon, to which the whole form was invited. She was a popular girl and everyone bought her presents, some expensive and some not so expensive. Carlotta gave her a beautiful book on horses, which she was absolutely delighted with, and the twins clubbed together to buy her an enormous bottle of bubble bath.

'So that you can soak away your aches and pains after a long day in the saddle,' laughed Isabel.

'I'm afraid I'm broke this week,' said Bobby handing

the girl a small box of chocolates. 'But happy birthday anyway, Libby.'

'Thanks awfully, Bobby,' said Libby happily, accepting the chocolates with as much pleasure as if they had been the crown jewels. 'I don't think I've ever received so many presents in my life. Thank you everyone. What a lovely birthday this is!'

And what a great party they had. First there were riotous games in the garden, then tea in the big kitchen. There were cries of 'ooh' and 'ah' as the girls gazed happily at the plates piled high with cakes, biscuits and sandwiches of every kind.

'This is what I call a party!' exclaimed Bobby in delight. 'Thanks a lot, Mrs Francis.'

The others echoed this and Libby's mother said with a smile, 'Well, just make sure you eat up every scrap of it! I don't want to see a single crumb left on these plates.'

'No problem there, Mrs Francis,' laughed Hilary. And indeed there wasn't. The girls were very hungry indeed after their energetic games and attacked the food as though they hadn't eaten in days. Libby's mother kept their glasses filled with lemonade and the party was a great success.

'Can I help you to clear away, Mrs Francis?' offered Alison politely, once tea was over.

'That's kind of you, dear, but go and enjoy yourself outside with the others,' said Libby's mother, smiling at the girl. This was the first time Mrs Francis had met Fern's friend, Alison, and she had taken a great liking to her.

Alison was like her niece in many ways, yet she had a gentle, kindly side to her nature which Fern lacked. Mrs Francis was fond of her niece, but she wasn't blind to the girl's faults, which worried her at times. It would be a good thing, she thought, if some of Alison rubbed off on Fern.

'What shall we do now?' asked Libby, once the girls were outside again.

'I don't feel like doing much of anything after that lovely tea,' said Janet, flopping down on the grass. 'I'm quite happy to just laze in the sun and chat.'

Everyone seemed to feel the same, settling down and stretching out comfortably.

'Wouldn't it be brilliant if we could do this every Saturday?' sighed Doris happily.

'Well, Isabel and I have a birthday coming up after half-term,' said Pat. 'Mum and Daddy have promised us some money, and I bet Miss Theobald would give permission for us to have a party in the common-room.'

'Who needs permission?' scoffed Bobby. 'I vote we make it a midnight feast.'

Several voices cried out excitedly.

'What a wonderful idea!'

'A feast! Oh, yes, let's!'

'It would be fun,' agreed Isabel. 'But we can't! Libby and Fern wouldn't be able to come, and I'd feel really mean about leaving them out, especially after Libby was decent enough to invite us all here today.'

Everyone agreed to this at once, but Bobby said wickedly, 'Who said anything about leaving them out? It's only a few minutes' walk from here to St Clare's, and the moon will be up. I'm sure we could work out a way for Fern and Libby to join the feast without them being caught.'

Surprisingly it was the bold Carlotta, usually ripe for any kind of prank, who sounded a note of caution. 'I'm not so sure that's a good idea. It would be bad enough the rest of us being caught. But if it was discovered that the day girls were missing from their home in the middle of the night, the cat really *would* be among the pigeons!'

'Well, it won't be discovered,' said Janet with a scornful laugh. 'We'll make sure of that. Honestly, Carlotta, you seem to have lost your sense of fun since you became head of the form.'

'I haven't!' said Carlotta hotly, rather hurt by Janet's words. 'But I could lose my position if anything went wrong.'

'Perhaps Carlotta doesn't want us at the feast,' suggested Fern slyly. She had suddenly thought of a way to cause more trouble for Carlotta and, in order to make her plan work, it was vital that she and Libby be invited to the midnight feast.

'That's not true,' protested Carlotta unhappily, hating having to be a wet blanket. 'I'd love you both to come. It's just that as head girl . . .'

'Now let's get this clear,' broke in Janet. 'Are we to understand that if Hilary was still head girl, you would have no objection to the day girls coming to our feast?'

'That's right,' said Carlotta with a frown, wondering where this was leading. She soon found out.

'I see,' said Janet smoothly. 'So you would have been

quite prepared to allow Hilary to jeopardize her position, but now that you are head, you aren't prepared to take any risks. Rather hypocritical, Carlotta, if you ask me.'

'Oh, Janet, that's a bit strong,' protested Pat. 'A hypocrite is one thing Carlotta has never been.'

'Why, Pat, how can you say that?' put in Fern, eager to back up Janet against a girl she saw as her enemy. 'Remember when you, Isabel and Carlotta stopped here on your way to school that first day? Carlotta actually mentioned the possibility of us attending a midnight feast then! But, of course, that was before she found out that she was to be head girl. Libby, what do you say? You'd like to go to the feast, wouldn't you?'

Poor Libby didn't know *what* to say! On the one hand she badly wanted to go to the feast. On the other, she didn't want to go against her friend.

Carlotta, who had been looking grave and thoughtful, saved her from having to answer. Her firm little chin up, she said in her frank way, 'Fern and Janet are quite right. I *have* been a hypocrite, although I didn't see it that way. I just thought that I was being a responsible head girl. Yes, Janet, I would have been prepared to let Hilary risk her position if she was in my place. And yes, Fern, you're right about what I said on that first day. So, girls, you are both very welcome at the feast and if – Heaven forbid – anything should go wrong and we're caught, I shall take full responsibility.' Carlotta grinned suddenly, looking more like herself as her dark eyes twinkled merrily. 'After all, if I *am* dropped as head girl, it won't be the end of the world!'

'Good for you, Carlotta!' called out Doris.

'Yes! And nothing will go wrong – touch wood,' said Isabel, tapping Doris on the head.

'Here, do you mind?' said Doris, with a comical expression.

Everyone laughed, then Pat spoke.

'Janet, I think you ought to take back what you said about Carlotta being a hypocrite. She's been big enough to admit that she got a bit muddle-headed about things. Now *you* should be big enough to admit that you were wrong about her.'

'Of course,' said Janet at once, turning a little red. Carlotta's forthright speech had taken the wind out of her sails a bit. It was difficult to hold a grudge in the face of such straightforward honesty. Never one to shirk an unpleasant task, Janet said bluntly, 'I take it back, Carlotta. You're no hypocrite.' Then, grinning ruefully, she held out her hand. 'No hard feelings?'

'None at all,' agreed Carlotta, returning both the grin and the handshake.

Inwardly, though, neither girl felt quite so sure. A truce had been agreed, but it was an uneasy one. Pat and Isabel discussed the matter in a quiet corner of the common-room later.

'I can see a terrific row brewing between Janet and Carlotta,' said Isabel worriedly. 'Yet they've always been such good pals up to now. I just can't understand what's gone wrong between them.'

Nor could Pat. 'I wish they would just have a blazing row and clear the air once and for all,' she sighed. 'I hate all this bad feeling in the atmosphere.'

The incident was on Carlotta's mind too when she went to bed that night, making it difficult for her to sleep. Despite her bold talk this afternoon, she was more worried than she cared to admit about the two day girls coming to the proposed feast. It wouldn't be the end of the world if she was no longer head girl, she had said defiantly. But, in reality, she would be deeply upset and feel a complete failure. She had written a long and excited letter to her father and grandmother at the beginning of term, telling them her exciting news. And they had written straight back, letting Carlotta know how proud and delighted they were. How bitterly disappointed in her they would be if this important and responsible position was taken from her!

11

Half-term

Before plans could be made for the twins' birthday feast, there was the excitement of half-term. The third formers were up with the lark that day, fighting good-naturedly for the bathrooms before arraying themselves in their prettiest summer dresses.

'Are your parents coming to take you out, Rachel?' asked Hilary, secretly rather hoping that they were. Like most of the others, she was dying to see the famous actors in person.

'Yes, and Alison will be joining us as her parents are away.'

'Won't they be proud of you when they hear all about the play you've written!' said Bobby.

'The play?' Rachel looked blank for a moment, then said rather stiffly, 'I don't suppose I shall tell them about it.'

'Funny girl,' remarked Pat to her twin as Rachel moved away. 'I don't know quite what to make of her. At the start of term I thought she was dreadfully stuck up and conceited, then she seemed to settle down and become one of us. But she still goes all cold and distant at times.'

'Oh, never mind about Rachel,' cried Isabel, who was in high spirits. 'I'm just looking forward to seeing our own parents! Hey, Gladys, I bet you're dying to see your mum again!'

'I'll say!' answered the girl with her gentle smile. 'We're going out to lunch at a hotel with Mirabel and her parents, so it should be good fun.'

Just then Carlotta came into the common-room, looking most unlike herself – but extremely pretty – in a lovely pale blue dress, a matching ribbon confining her unruly curls.

'Hello, who's this elegant stranger?' joked Doris. 'Can we help you, young lady?'

'Idiot!' laughed Carlotta, aiming a playful punch at Doris. Then she straightened the skirt of her dress and said self-consciously, 'I don't feel like *me* at all.'

'What's this in aid of, Carlotta?' asked Hilary with a grin. 'You wouldn't be trying to impress your grand-mother, by any chance?'

'I would,' answered the girl frankly. 'You know how she always complains that I look wild and untidy. I thought that if I wore the dress she bought me for my last birthday, I might stand a chance of getting into her good books.'

'Any particular reason why you want to get into her good books?' asked Pat, amused.

'Actually, it's all for you and Isabel,' answered Carlotta with a grin. 'You see, the more grandmother approves of me, the more generous she becomes. So the size of your birthday present, twins, all depends on how ladylike I am!'

Isabel winked at her twin, saying, 'Well, if Pat and I get a stick of toffee between us, we'll know that you've misbehaved, so just mind your Ps and Qs.'

Everybody laughed, then Mirabel cried, 'Oh, look, a car has just pulled up outside! It's the first lot of parents!'

Immediately everyone rushed to the window, Doris putting her head out and calling excitedly, 'They're mine! Hi, Mum! Dad!'

'Steady on, or you'll fall out of the window and squash your poor mother flat!' laughed Janet, pulling her back.

But Doris didn't care. 'Come on!' she called out to Hilary, who was spending the day with her. 'Let's go and say hi!'

The cars arrived thick and fast after that, until the lawn was crowded with people.

'I'm rather nervous about meeting your parents,' Alison confided to Rachel.

'Why?' laughed the girl. 'They don't have two heads each, you know.'

'No, but they're famous,' said Alison rather gravely. 'They're bound to think I'm a little nobody.'

'What nonsense!' cried Rachel. 'Their faces might be famous, but my folks are just normal down-to-earth people – and here they are! Come on, Alison, and you'll see for yourself.'

Sure enough, Rachel's parents were extremely pleasant and friendly, not at all up in the air as Alison had feared, and she relaxed at once in their company. Unfortunately, Alison's decision to spend the day with Rachel had caused some coolness between herself and Fern.

Fern had asked Alison prettily if she would care to spend half-term with her. 'We'll have lunch at home,' she had said. 'Then afterwards we'll come over to St Clare's to watch the tennis and swimming and take a look at the art exhibition.'

'Oh, Fern, that's awfully kind of you, but I'm afraid I've already agreed to go out with Rachel and her parents,' Alison had replied dismayed, for she always hated to hurt anyone's feelings.

'Well, surely you can tell her that you've changed your mind,' Fern had said.

'But that would be terribly rude after she asked me first. Besides, I haven't changed my mind! I want to go out with Rachel.'

'I see,' Fern had said coldly. Then she gave the high little laugh that had begun to irritate Alison. 'I suppose the truth is that you just want to rub shoulders with her famous parents!'

'That's a terrible thing to say!' gasped Alison, feeling hurt. 'Of course I'm looking forward to meeting them, but my main reason for going is because Rachel is my friend and I like her.'

'As if anyone could like that stuck-up creature!' snapped Fern. 'Well, do as you please, Alison. I shall find someone else to spend the day with.' Then Fern had turned on her heel and stalked away.

She had made it up with Alison later, but there was still some tension between the two girls. When Alison had asked her if she had found someone to spend the day with her, Fern had given a curious little smile and said, 'Oh, yes. Someone very interesting.'

'Who?' Alison had asked curiously.

But Fern would only shake her head and give an infuriatingly smug smile. Alison knew that all of the other third formers had made arrangements of their own, and Fern didn't have any friends in another form, so she simply couldn't imagine who the girl's mystery guest could be.

She found out that afternoon. Rachel's parents were deep in conversation with Miss Adams when Alison spotted the Francis family arriving. Libby immediately took her parents and brother to meet Carlotta's father, while Fern made straight for Alison and Rachel. With her was a tall, fair girl, whom Alison had never seen before. She nudged Rachel.

'Here comes Fern. I wonder who that is with her? She looks rather nice.'

Rachel glanced across – and the colour drained from her cheeks, leaving her white as a sheet, eyes wide with horror.

'Why, Rachel, whatever is the matter?' cried Alison, alarmed. 'Do you feel all right?'

Rachel did not answer, unable to move or speak as Fern and her companion came over.

'Alison – and Rachel!' said Fern in her sweetest, most gushing tone. She was wearing her brightest smile too, realized Rachel bitterly – and unless she was mistaken, there was more than a hint of spite in it.

'Alison, I'd like you to meet an old friend of mine, Sara Jameson. Of course, there's no need to introduce her to you, Rachel, because she's an old friend of yours as well.'

'Really? Do you two know one another?' asked Alison, looking at Rachel in surprise. 'Oh, of course, I remember! Sara is the girl who was at drama school with you! Well, how nice for you both to meet again.'

Rachel didn't seem to take any pleasure in the meeting at all, though. Her tone was odd and stilted as she said, 'Hello, Sara. What brings you to these parts?'

'Oh, my grandmother lives near here and I've been staying with her for a while. When Fern found out I was in the area she asked me to spend half-term with her. Wasn't that nice of her?' If Sara found anything peculiar in Rachel's behaviour she didn't betray it, her own manner open and friendly. 'How are you settling in here?' she asked warmly. 'I must say, it looks a really nice school.'

'It is . . . I . . . I'm fine here,' answered Rachel disjointedly, looking wildly around as though trying to escape. Alison couldn't imagine what had got into her. Suddenly Rachel grabbed her arm and said hastily, 'Oh, Mum and Dad are calling us! Come on, Alison. Goodbye, Fern. Sara – nice to see you again.' Then Alison found herself being propelled across the lawn, only to find that Sir Robert and Lady Helen were still talking with Miss Adams.

'Rachel, whatever is the matter with you?' said Alison, unusually waspishly. She would have liked to spend a little longer with Fern and Sara, who she had thought a very pleasant girl. She gave Rachel a narrow, sideways glance. Surely *Sara* couldn't be behind the odd way her friend was acting?

Lady Helen happened to turn round and, putting her arm round her daughter's shoulders, said with her dazzling smile, 'Is everything all right, darling?'

'Fine, Mum,' said Rachel, her answering smile a little forced. 'Everything's just fine.'

But everything wasn't fine, thought Alison with a puzzled frown. Something had happened to upset Rachel terribly. If only she could discover what it was and help her friend.

Fern could have enlightened her! Over the half-term break, Sara, unwittingly, told her everything that she needed to know. Just having the knowledge, knowing that Rachel would see it in her eyes, gave Fern a feeling of power and that was all she wanted. It is quite likely that she would have said nothing to the rest of the third form about it if a dreadful quarrel hadn't sprung up between Rachel and herself during rehearsals after the break.

A bad day for Rachel

Carlotta was finding Rachel a great help with rehearsals. She had a keen eye for detail and often spotted something that Carlotta overlooked. 'If Bobby made her entrance from the other side, she wouldn't overshadow Gladys so much,' she would suggest. Or, 'Mirabel's excellent, but it really isn't necessary for her to roar like that! If she spoke normally her performance would be far more effective.'

'I sometimes think that you should be directing instead of me,' Carlotta said one day.

Rachel had blushed and said with a laugh, 'I don't know about that, but I think it's easier for me because I visualized the play in my mind as I wrote it, so I can instantly spot anything I think isn't quite right.'

Carlotta bit her lip. Not for the first time it occurred to her that it really *would* be better for the third form if Rachel took over altogether. Yet the girls had chosen her and if she simply handed the reins to Rachel, some of them – Janet in particular – would accuse her of shirking her responsibilities.

Then, quite suddenly, the matter was taken completely out of her hands.

It was a Saturday afternoon and Carlotta was out

riding with Libby, while the other third formers were at a loose end.

'If only Carlotta was here to direct, we could fit in another rehearsal,' said Doris.

'Well, why shouldn't we rehearse just because Carlotta is too busy with her own interests?' cried Janet suddenly. 'Libby doesn't have any lines, so we shan't miss her, and Rachel can step in as director. Rachel, what do you say?'

'Well, I don't mind, so long as Carlotta doesn't think I'm treading on her toes,' answered Rachel.

'Nonsense!' said Janet. 'Anyway it's Carlotta's own fault. She spends more time at Libby's these days than she does at St Clare's.

Fern, who had come over to the school to spend the afternoon with Alison, smiled and said sweetly, 'Yes, let Rachel take over. I'm sure that with her drama school background she'll do a marvellous job.'

Alison gave Fern an approving smile. The girl really was making an effort to get on better with Rachel. Only Rachel herself saw the sly look in Fern's big blue eyes and heard the spite behind the sweetness. Bobby sped along to Miss Theobald to get permission for the third formers to use the hall, and soon a rehearsal was in full swing.

Everything went swimmingly until it came to Fern's part. The girl was playing a maid and only had one line, but she persisted in muffing it. And Rachel was quite certain that she was only doing it to annoy her, especially when Fern kept directing smug, knowing little smiles in her direction. Rachel tried hard to keep her temper, taking the girl through the line time and time again, resisting the impulse to yell at her. But really, Fern would try the patience of a saint.

The explosion came when Janet, who along with some of the others was becoming impatient, called out, 'For Heaven's sake, let's move on to another scene or we shall have wasted a whole afternoon on Fern. Come on, Rachel, you're supposed to be in charge.'

'Oh, do let me have just one more try at it,' pleaded Fern. 'I promise to get it right this time.'

'Very well,' agreed Rachel through clenched teeth. 'But this is positively the last time.'

So yet again Fern spoke her line. And yet again she got it wrong. It was just too much for Rachel. 'For goodness' sake, how difficult can it be to learn one line?' she shouted, clenching her fists tightly at her sides. 'You're the worst actress I have ever seen! Well, Fern, I'm sacking you! You can swap parts with Libby and take her non-speaking role. At least she has the brains to string a few words together!'

'You can't do that!' protested Fern furiously, turning red. 'Only Carlotta can! You're just standing in for her, so don't get too big for your boots, Rachel.'

'Then I shall suggest it to Carlotta, and I'm pretty sure she will agree with me,' said Rachel, adding with a sneer, 'She shares my opinion that you can't act to save your life.'

There was silence for a moment, the third formers watching with bated breath as Fern glared down poisonously at Rachel from the stage. They waited for her to burst into tears, or flounce off. To their surprise Fern did neither of these things. Instead she gave a scornful laugh and said coolly, 'Well, you would know all about being a poor actress, wouldn't you? That's why you were sent away from drama school. Not because you were taking time off to be an ordinary schoolgirl, but because they didn't want you there any more – because you just can't act!'

Rachel said nothing, but turned very pale and trembled from head to foot. This was what she had dreaded. Now the others would know what a fraud she was!

Fern went on in that smooth, hateful little voice, 'Sara told me all about it at half-term. About how the principal of the drama school had to tell your parents that you would never follow in their footsteps and they would do better to take you away and send you to an ordinary school. And you thought that you could come here and lord it over all of us, didn't you? The great actress! Ha!'

Unable to bear Fern's triumphant expression any longer, and not daring to look at the faces of the others for fear of the contempt she would see there, Rachel gave a sob and fled from the hall.

'Well, now you all know what a fraud she is,' said Fern, looking round at the others. 'What do you think of your precious Rachel now, Alison?' She stopped suddenly, for there *was* contempt in the others' faces. But it wasn't for Rachel. It was for her.

'That was a rotten thing to do!' said Alison in a

trembling voice. 'Fern, how could you?'

'I'll say it was rotten,' said Hilary scornfully. 'And cunning! You deliberately provoked Rachel into losing her temper, just so that you could blurt this out in front of us all.'

'I didn't!' wailed Fern, horrified at the reaction her bombshell had produced, with even Alison turning against her. 'If she hadn't said that she was going to sack me, I would have kept quiet.'

'Perhaps, but you've just loved having a hold over Rachel, haven't you?' snapped Alison disdainfully. 'I've known something was wrong ever since you brought Sara here at half-term.'

'I don't know why you're all so angry with me!' protested Fern. 'You should be grateful to me for exposing her.'

'Yes, that's exactly what you've done,' said Pat coldly. 'Exposed her and torn away the protective shell Rachel had built up round herself. Can't you imagine how dreadful this business must have been for her? The poor girl must have been absolutely shattered when she was told that she had no future on the stage.'

'Not to mention the shame of her parents being told that the school no longer wanted her,' put in Isabel. 'She must have felt that she had let them down terribly.'

'And she was settling in here so well,' said Gladys. 'Admittedly she was a bit full of herself at first, but now we know it was just an act, her way of coping with what had happened. Since we all praised her for writing the play, she's really become one of us.'

'Yes, and you didn't like that, did you, Fern? Especially when she began getting closer to Alison,' sneered Janet. 'Now clear out! We've all had quite enough of you and your spite for one day.'

Shocked, Fern turned a pleading look on Alison who glared at her and said, 'Go away, Fern. I shall have to think carefully about whether or not I still want to be your friend after this.' She turned her back and Fern, just as Rachel had done earlier, gave a sob and ran out.

'Wasn't that just awful!' said Doris, looking unusually grave. 'I wonder where Rachel went?'

'Probably up to the dormitory,' said Hilary. 'One of us really should go and see if she's all right.'

'I'll go,' said Alison. 'After all, she is my friend.' Then, quite suddenly, she put her hands up to her face and began to cry.

'Poor Rachel!' she sobbed. 'I feel so sorry for her.'

Janet gave her a pat on the shoulder. 'Never mind, Alison. She'll be all right once she knows none of us thinks any the less of her. All the same, I don't think you're going to be a great comfort if you mean to cry all over her.'

Alison gave a watery little laugh and Isabel said, 'Carlotta really ought to be the one to deal with this, as head of the form.'

'Yes, but, as usual, Carlotta isn't around when she's needed,' said Janet drily. 'I'll go and have a word with Rachel.'

Everyone agreed to this at once. Janet might be a little sharp tongued at times, but she was good hearted and had plenty of common sense. She would need both of those qualities in dealing with poor, miserable Rachel.

Another row

Janet found Rachel in the dormitory, curled up into a tight little ball and absolutely sobbing her heart out. Feeling desperately sorry for her, Janet went across and laid a hand on her shoulder.

'Leave me alone!' cried the girl, shrugging her off.

'I can't leave you like this,' said Janet calmly, sitting down beside her. 'Come on, Rachel! It's never any good bottling things up. You'll feel much better if you talk about it.'

'Oh, yes, I bet you'd just love to hear all the details of my humiliation,' stormed Rachel through her tears. 'So that you can go back and tell the others and you can all have a good laugh at me!'

'Rachel, that just isn't true!' cried Janet, shocked. 'I just want to help you. We all do.'

Rachel stopped crying for a moment and looked into the girl's warm brown eyes, feeling comforted when she saw the compassion there. Taking a deep breath she said, 'There isn't much to tell. You know it all, thanks to Fern. All my great talk of becoming an actress was empty. Last term the principal took me aside and told me – very kindly – that I just didn't have enough talent and that I would be better off setting my sights on a different career.'

'I see,' said Janet solemnly. 'That must have been shattering. But, Rachel, you should have been straight with us from the start. We would have understood.'

'I know, but I couldn't bring myself to accept it,' sighed Rachel. 'That's why I put on that stupid, conceited, stuck-up act when I first came here. Because I still desperately wanted to believe that I could be an actress. I just couldn't come to terms with the fact that I had failed and let my parents down.'

'Were they terribly disappointed?' asked Janet gently.

'They've been marvellous,' answered Rachel. 'They've told me that anything I want to do is fine by them, and they'll give me all the support they can.'

'Well, you're very lucky to have a mother and father like that,' said Janet warmly. 'And I suppose it's better for you to know the truth sooner rather than later.'

Rachel gave her an impatient look and sniffed. 'Oh, I couldn't expect you to understand! The theatre is in my blood! I've grown up with it as a big part of my life and I always expected my future to lie there.'

'Perhaps it still does,' said Janet thoughtfully. 'You just need to approach it from a different angle.'

'Whatever do you mean?' asked Rachel, curious in spite of herself.

'Rachel, you have *enormous* talent,' Janet told her earnestly. 'Not as an actress, but as a writer. This play you've written for the third is just brilliant – and you're not half bad as a director either. If you concentrate on those things, I really think you could have a big future in the theatre.'

Rachel stared at the girl for a moment, then gasped, 'Janet, do you really think so?'

'I *know* so!' laughed Janet. 'But don't take my word for it – ask Miss Adams. I overheard her talking to the head after she had looked in on our rehearsal the other day.'

'Yes?' prompted Rachel, eagerly. 'What did she say?'

But Janet shook her head and grinned. 'I'm not going to tell you, my girl, because I don't want you getting swollen headed! All I will say is that she shares my opinion.'

Rachel gave a shaky laugh. 'I can't quite believe this! Do you know, for the first time since leaving the academy I feel that my future isn't looking quite so bleak. Thanks, Janet.'

Janet grinned. 'Glad to have been of help. Now, how about coming back to rehearsal. Hey, won't your parents be thrilled when they come to see our play and find out that it's been written by you?'

'Yes, but . . .' Rachel bit her lip. 'Janet, I can't face everyone just yet. Fern . . .'

'Fern has gone,' said Janet, her face hardening. 'Everyone is absolutely disgusted with her and told her so in no uncertain terms.'

'Honestly? Even Alison?'

'*Especially* Alison!' Janet assured her. 'You have a very loyal friend there. Now listen, Rachel, I've been thinking. You have much more flair for directing than Carlotta so, if it's all right with you, I'm going to suggest that she lets you take over completely.'

'Oh, but I couldn't push Carlotta out like that!' exclaimed Rachel. 'It just wouldn't be fair.'

'To be honest, I don't think Carlotta will mind,' said Janet. 'It will give her more time to spend riding, which is all she really seems interested in.'

'But what about you?' asked Rachel, looking at Janet curiously. 'You only lost out to Carlotta as director by one vote, remember. If anyone takes over it should be you.'

'I wouldn't do nearly as good a job as you, and I see that now,' said Janet with her usual frankness. 'Well, Rachel? What do you say?'

Rachel gave a laugh, a genuinely delighted one this time. 'I really would love to do it,' she said. 'But only if Carlotta agrees.'

'Good,' said Janet. 'I'll speak to her about it as soon as she gets back.'

What a pity that Janet didn't use the same tact in dealing with Carlotta as she had with Rachel! When Carlotta returned, she said to her, 'Could I have a quick word with you in the common-room?'

'So long as it *is* quick,' answered Carlotta. 'I'm starving!'

The common-room was empty when the two girls entered, most of the third form having gone in to tea.

'Well, you certainly missed some excitement this afternoon,' began Janet, and quickly explained about the quarrel between Fern and Rachel.

Carlotta listened, astonished, and exclaimed at the end, 'Well! What a spiteful creature Fern is! And poor Rachel! Is she all right?'

'She is now,' said Janet, and repeated the conversation she had had with Rachel.

'Well, Janet, I think you gave her some very sound advice,' said Carlotta sincerely. 'Good for you!'

'Thanks,' said Janet. 'Look, you don't mind us holding a spur-of-the-moment rehearsal without you?'

'Of course not,' laughed Carlotta. 'I'm sure that Rachel stood in for me admirably.'

'She did,' said Janet, giving Carlotta a narrow look. 'More than admirably. The thing is, Carlotta, we've decided – Rachel and I – that it might be better if she took over from you as director.'

Carlotta felt dismayed and a little angry when she heard this. It was true that she had been thinking about giving Rachel the job. But it was one thing for her to make the decision – quite another to have it taken out of her hands like this. 'Well!' she exclaimed. 'You *have* been busy while my back has been turned. Have you been plotting anything else against me that I ought to know about?'

'Oh, Carlotta, don't be so melodramatic,' laughed Janet. 'No one's plotting against you! We just want what's best for the play. Surely you want the same?'

'Of course,' agreed Carlotta stiffly. 'But I'd like to have been consulted, rather than told what has already been decided. Really, Janet, anyone would think that *you* were head of the form!'

Janet flushed a little and said coldly, 'Well, you can't blame me if I sometimes forget that *you* are. You don't seem to care about anything except enjoying yourself over at Libby's house. You should have been the one to comfort Rachel this afternoon but, as you weren't here, I had to step in.'

'It's not true that I don't care about anything!' cried Carlotta, taken aback and feeling very angry. 'How was I to know that a quarrel would spring up this afternoon? I think you're being most unreasonable, Janet.'

Then it suddenly occurred to Carlotta that she would not be involved in the third's play at all. She hadn't bothered auditioning for any of the parts as she had assumed that she would have her hands full with directing. Now that was being taken away from her and she – head of the form – was to be completely left out of the play. 'I shouldn't be surprised if you planned this just to push me out,' she said wildly. 'You haven't backed me up in anything this term, and you've lost no opportunity to undermine me.'

'What nonsense!' cried Janet, though she couldn't help feeling a bit ashamed. She *hadn't* backed up Carlotta as she should have but somehow she hadn't been able to help herself, letting these horrible, jealous feelings take hold. 'You can take Fern's part,' she offered, in a conciliatory tone but Carlotta, in a fine temper now, brushed this aside, snapping, 'I thought *Rachel* was going to direct, not you! Surely that should be her decision – or do you intend to issue your orders through her?'

Janet's eyes glittered angrily, all thoughts of reconciliation forgotten, as she glared at Carlotta. And into this tense situation walked Rachel herself. She realized at once that she had interrupted a row and said awkwardly, 'Sorry. I was just looking for Alison.'

'I expect she's gone in to tea,' said Janet. 'Which is what I intend to do, instead of wasting my time here.' And, throwing one last glare at Carlotta, she left the room.

Carlotta reminded herself that she had no quarrel with Rachel, putting on a wide smile and saying brightly, 'So, you are to be our new director! Congratulations!'

'Well, it was really Janet's idea,' faltered Rachel, seeing straight through Carlotta's forced, jolly manner to the hurt beneath. 'I told her that I would only consider it if you didn't mind. But you mind terribly, don't you, Carlotta? That's why you and Janet were rowing. This is just what I was afraid would happen! I'll go to Janet at once and tell her that I intend to stand down.'

'You'll do nothing of the sort!' cried Carlotta, giving Rachel a clap on the shoulder, all the fight going out of her. 'Janet and I don't see eye to eye about very much these days, but we agree that you're the right girl for the job.'

'Well, if you're absolutely sure?' said Rachel, still a little uncertain.

'I am,' Carlotta assured her. 'By the way, I'm sorry about what happened with Fern today, and sorrier still that I wasn't here to deal with her! Don't worry, though, I shall see to it personally that she apologizes to you.'

Rachel gave a laugh. 'Actually, Fern has done me a favour although she didn't mean to. I feel much more comfortable now that my dark secret is out!'

'I'm glad,' said Carlotta sincerely. But she was determined that Fern would apologize. She might not be director of the play any more, but Carlotta was still head girl and meant to have her way over this!

An apology – and a birthday

Fern did apologize to Rachel. Not because of anything Carlotta said to her or because she felt that she had done anything wrong. Simply, she felt she had to make things right with Alison, who had treated her very coldly since the fateful rehearsal. As Pat said to her twin, 'At least something good has come out of this awful business and Alison sees Fern for what she really is.'

Isabel had nodded. 'Poor Alison. I think she was quite shocked to discover what a spiteful little cat Fern can be.'

Alison *had* been shocked. Silly and feather-headed she might be, but there was no spite in her nature, and she had been truly dismayed by Fern's behaviour.

On Monday morning Fern arrived at school early, waylaying Rachel as she came out of the dining-room after breakfast, and offering her a prettily worded apology.

Rachel accepted it graciously and several of the third formers, who were present, thawed towards Fern a little, feeling that at least she had been decent enough to try to put things right. Alison made things up with her because she really did enjoy having someone to chatter with about fashions and hair-dos, things that Rachel wasn't at all interested in. Yet, somehow, the two girls couldn't quite get back on their old footing. Something had gone out of their friendship, realized Alison sadly, and she didn't know whether it would ever come back again. Still, Alison had to give Fern full marks for trying. The girl really seemed determined to make everyone forget her cattiness, behaving most pleasantly to all the third formers – even Carlotta – over the next few days, and being particularly sweet to Rachel.

When Doris, who was quite broke, needed some money to have her tennis-racket mended, it was Fern who lent it to her. Then when Gladys went down with flu and had to be dropped from an important school tennis match, Fern was the first to visit her in the sickbay. Even when Rachel, who felt that she had to back up Janet, informed Fern rather awkwardly that Carlotta would now be taking over her role in the play, Fern took it well. The others expected sulks and tantrums, perhaps even tears, but Fern said warmly, and with a charming smile, 'I'm sure that Carlotta will be excellent in the part. Perhaps I could help out backstage on the night, with make-up and hairdressing? I'm quite good at that kind of thing, if I do say so myself.'

'Thanks, Fern,' said Rachel, surprised and pleased by how well the girl had taken the news. 'That will be a big help.'

'I must say, Fern really is behaving very well over all this,' said Bobby to Janet. 'Perhaps we've misjudged her a bit.'

Janet, who could be very shrewd and far-seeing,

wasn't so sure. 'There's just something about her I don't trust,' she said. 'Still, perhaps I'm wrong. Only time will tell!'

Soon it was the twins' birthday and the third got down to the thrilling business of planning the birthday feast.

'Let's get out the hamper that Mum gave us at half-term,' said Isabel. 'Then we can see exactly what we've got and what else we need to buy.'

The rest of the form gathered round in anticipation as the twins opened the large box.

'Wow! Look at all these goodies,' exclaimed Doris. 'I should think there's enough here for two midnight feasts!'

'Tinned prawns!' cried Janet ecstatically. 'My favourite.'

'And tuna, pineapple, fruit cake,' said Hilary. 'And don't these chocolates look delicious!'

'Our gran's sent us some money so that we can buy a lovely big birthday cake, too,' said Pat happily.

'Well, we others ought to contribute something,' said Bobby. 'It's only fair. Janet and I will buy the lemonade.'

'And I'll get some candles for the cake,' offered Mirabel.

One by one all the girls agreed to bring something for the feast and Rachel said, 'Now the only thing to decide is where and when.'

'When is easy,' said Isabel. 'Friday, because that's when our birthday is. Should we hold it in one of the dormitories?'

'The common-room would be better,' said Carlotta. 'Because it's further away from the mistresses' rooms and we shall be able to talk quite normally instead of whispering.'

'I can't tell you how much I'm looking forward to it,' said Libby, hugging herself. 'My party was fun, but a secret midnight affair with no grown-ups around will be too marvellous for words.'

'Have you and Fern worked out how you're going to get away?' asked Janet.

'It'll be as easy as pie,' said Fern confidently. 'Our room is at the other end of the landing from Aunt Polly and Uncle Tom's, and they both sleep like logs. We'll sneak down the stairs and out of the back door.'

'Yes, Mum and Dad sleep at the front of the house, so there's no fear of us waking them,' added Libby. 'We'll leave the door on the latch so that we can get back in again. My brother is awfully jealous about the feast, because nothing like this ever happens at his day school.'

'You surely haven't told your brother about it?' said Janet. 'I hope he can keep a secret. Mine is the most awful blabbermouth.'

'Will won't say a word,' Libby assured her. 'He's a good sport. Mind you, I may have to bribe him with a piece of birthday cake!'

'I dare say we can spare one,' laughed Pat. 'Only a few days to go! I can hardly wait!'

All of the girls found time to go into town over the next couple of days to buy everything that was needed for the feast. The twins hid all the goodies in a little cupboard near the common-room.

'It makes my mouth water just to look at all this marvellous food,' said Isabel. 'Oh, look, sausage rolls! How wonderful! I always say that a feast isn't a proper feast without sausage rolls.'

The day before the party, Fern came up to Pat carrying a large tin. 'Aunt Polly has been baking,' she explained. 'And she said that I could have some cakes for your party. Oh, I didn't tell her it was going to be a midnight one, of course. She thinks it will be a tea-time affair.'

'Great!' said Pat, removing the lid from the tin and looking at the little cakes with their pink and white icing. 'These look scrumptious. Thanks, Fern – and do say thank you to your aunt as well.'

'Of course,' said Fern pleasantly. 'I'm really looking forward to this feast, Pat.'

This was quite true. But she wasn't looking forward to it in quite the same way as the other third formers were. For Fern meant to spoil the feast! She had worked out a cunning plan and was confident that no one would ever suspect she had anything to do with it, especially as she had behaved so well lately. And if everything went just as she hoped, Carlotta would not be head girl for much longer. At the very least she was sure to lose her privileges and be confined to school for some time. That in itself would be something, thought Fern, for at least she wouldn't keep popping over to the Oaks and sucking up to her aunt and uncle, not to mention Will. Whatever happened, Fern was determined to emerge the victor from this little episode.

Two girls were absent from school on the morning of the feast. One was Carlotta, who awoke with a dreadful sore throat and felt weak and shaky. She managed to make her way down to breakfast, but Miss Adams took one look at her and packed her straight off to Matron.

'You've got this horrid summer flu that's been going around,' said Matron after she had examined Carlotta and taken her temperature. 'A dose of medicine and a few days in bed for you, my girl.'

'Oh, Matron, no!' wailed Carlotta in dismay.

But Matron was already opening a large bottle of medicine and pouring out a spoonful, insisting that the girl swallow it.

'Ugh!' Carlotta grimaced. 'Horrible!'

'It will do you the world of good,' said Matron briskly. 'Now, get into your night things and straight into bed with you. This flu bug is very nasty, but it normally only lasts for a couple of days or so. With luck you could be back at school by Monday.' Carlotta did not move, staring at Matron in horror.

'Matron, I can't possibly spend the weekend in bed!' she cried. 'I'm going riding with Libby tomorrow, and I so much wanted to . . .' The girl broke off, biting her lip. She had almost let slip about the twins' feast.

'So much wanted to what?' prompted Matron.

'Oh . . . have a swim this afternoon.'

'A swim!' cried Matron, throwing up her hands in horror. 'With the dreadful cold you've got? Absolutely out of the question. Now, do as you're told, Carlotta.'

The girl sighed and gave in, knowing that it was useless to argue with Matron once she had made her mind up.

But why did she have to fall ill today of all days? It really was the most rotten luck!

The other invalid was Fern – though, in her case, the illness was feigned, a part of her carefully thought-out plan to spoil the third's feast.

'Goodness, you do look rather hot and flushed!' exclaimed Mrs Francis. Little did she know that the colour in her niece's cheeks had been brought on by excitement rather than illness.

'I really do feel terribly poorly,' moaned Fern. Indeed the third form, who had been so scathing about her acting talent, would have been quite astonished by her performance now. Her aunt was completely taken in, saying worriedly, 'Perhaps I should telephone the doctor.'

'Oh, no, Aunt Polly!' said Fern hastily. 'I'm sure that if I just spend the day quietly in bed I shall be all right.'

'Very well, dear,' said Mrs Francis. 'Libby, you can explain to Miss Adams that your cousin is unwell.'

Libby nodded and, once her mother had left the room, whispered, 'Fern, you'll miss the feast tonight. What a shame!'

'I know,' groaned Fern, as though she was genuinely disappointed. 'But I really do feel dreadful.'

After Libby had gone to school, Fern settled back against the pillows and picked up a book. What a long, dull day it was going to be with no one to talk to. But it would all be worth it in the end!

The third formers felt very sorry for the two absentees

but, on this, the twins' birthday, nothing could dampen their spirits for long. The twins were delighted with the presents they received from their friends and found it very hard to concentrate on their lessons. Of course, all of the mistresses knew that it was their birthday and tried to make allowances, but even the kind-hearted Mam'zelle flew into a rage when she spoke to Isabel three times without getting any response. The girl was gazing dreamily out of the window thinking pleasant thoughts about the night's feast, and didn't even hear the French mistress. At last Mirabel nudged her and Isabel looked round, startled, to find Mam'zelle glaring down at her.

'Oh, I beg your pardon. Were you speaking to me, Mam'zelle?' she asked.

'Three times have I spoken to you! And three times have you ignored me. I will not have it, Isabel. It is not like you to be so fluffy headed!'

'You mean *woolly* headed, Mam'zelle,' Hilary corrected her with a grin.

'Fluffy, woolly, what difference does it make?' said Mam'zelle impatiently. 'I know what you are thinking about, Isabel, you bad girl!'

Isabel stared at the Frenchwoman in alarm. How could she possibly know anything about the midnight feast?

'Ah, yes,' went on Mam'zelle. 'You think of birthday presents and cards. Yes, and a fine big cake with candles on it. Well, *ma petite*, there is a time for such thoughts and that time is not during my lesson, you understand?'

Relieved that Mam'zelle hadn't guessed about the feast after all, Isabel said meekly, 'Yes, Mam'zelle.' The girl did not dare let her attention wander after that, though it was most difficult. *How* she wished that midnight would come!

Midnight feast

At last midnight *did* come and Janet's little alarm clock, which she had placed beneath her pillow to muffle the noise, went off. She slipped out of bed and went round from one girl to another, whispering and shaking them gently.

'Midnight feast!'

'Come on, sleepyhead, it's time.'

'Bobby! Come on, Bobby, wake up!'

Then Pat crept into the dormitory next door and roused all the girls there. Soon they were making their way silently to the common-room. The twins, along with Bobby and Janet, fetched all the food from the cupboard, while Hilary slipped along to the side door where she was to wait for Libby and let her in. Fortunately she didn't have to wait very long and the two girls joined the others in the common-room.

'Ah, good, you made it!' said Pat to Libby.

'Yes, everyone was fast asleep when I left the house,' said Libby with a grin. 'And I'm starving, I can tell you. Mum thought I was sickening for something, too, when I refused seconds at tea today.'

'Well, let's tuck in,' said Isabel. 'Mirabel, start dishing

up, would you – and try not to make too many crumbs! Gladys, you can open that tin of tuna.'

Soon all the food was ready and the girls had the most marvellous feast!

'Mm, these prawns are delicious,' said Doris happily.

'So is this pineapple,' said Pat. 'Especially when you dip it in lemonade. Try it, Isabel.'

'What a pity that Carlotta and Fern are missing all the fun,' sighed Libby.

'Yes, it's tough luck on them,' said Isabel. 'Pat and I went to see Carlotta for a few minutes this afternoon and she was really down in the dumps. We promised to save her a slice of birthday cake, though, and that cheered her up a bit. We'll give you some to take back to Fern as well.'

'It's a good job that you bought such an enormous one,' said Alison, looking at the huge confection, covered in yellow icing and sugar roses. 'Don't forget that you've promised Will a slice too. Rachel, pour out some more lemonade and we'll drink a toast while the twins cut the cake.'

So the candles were lit and the twins blew them out and cut big slices of cake, while the form drank their health in lemonade.

'Happy birthday, twins!'

'And many more of them!'

While the third formers enjoyed their feast, Fern was out of bed too. Tiptoeing softly along the landing, she listened outside the door of her aunt and uncle's room for a moment. To her satisfaction, the only sound that came to her was a gentle snore from Uncle Tom. All was quiet in Will's room too, and Fern padded softly down the stairs. A pang of conscience smote her when she reached the sitting-room. It really was a shame that Libby and Alison had to be involved in this and would get into trouble as well. But her dislike and jealousy of Carlotta had reached the stage where she just had to do something about it and, if other people got hurt along the way, it was just too bad. Anyway, she would find a way of making it up to Libby and Alison somehow.

Fern didn't know, of course, that Carlotta was in the sickbay and wasn't even at the feast. If only she had known, what a lot of trouble she would have saved the third formers – and herself! Going to the telephone, she picked up the receiver and dialled a number.

Miss Theobald was away that evening and it was Mam'zelle, who often sat up late, who heard the telephone ringing in the head's study. '*Tiens*!' she exclaimed, startled. 'Who can be telephoning at this late hour?' She went into the study and lifted the receiver, saying sharply, ' 'Allo?'

'Miss Theobald?' came a deep, muffled voice from the other end of the line.

'Miss Theobald is not here,' said Mam'zelle. 'Can I give her a message?'

Fern recognized the French mistress's voice and grinned to herself. This was even better! Mam'zelle had a hot temper and was very strict indeed about the girls getting a good night's sleep and remaining in bed after lights out. This really spelt trouble for Carlotta!

'I thought you should know that the third form are having a feast in their common-room at this very minute,' said Fern in her disguised voice.

Mam'zelle gave a shocked gasp and demanded, 'Who are you? How do you know this?' But there was no reply, for Fern had gone, satisfied with what she had done.

Mam'zelle, meanwhile, screwed up her face in distaste, wondering who the cowardly, anonymous caller could have been. How she disliked such low, underhand people! But she also disliked this very English custom of midnight feasts. How could the girls be expected to do their best work if they were awake half the night? Ah, such a thing would never happen in her beloved France! Suddenly Mam'zelle remembered that it was the twins' birthday. She recalled, too, Isabel's inattention in class and the excitement that had seemed to be in the air that morning. Undoubtedly the caller had been telling the truth.

'*Méchantes filles*!' she said angrily under her breath before going out into the corridor. Ah, what a shock those wicked girls would get!

The feasters weren't the only ones in for a shock. For as Fern put the receiver down, a triumphant smile on her face, she heard a sound behind her and, turning sharply, came face to face with Will. It was obvious from the expression of disgust on his face that he had heard every word!

'You horrid little sneak!' he said scornfully. 'How could you do such a thing? To tell on your own cousin is just about the lowest thing I ever heard of.'

Fern turned paper white at the contempt in his tone and stammered, 'I never meant Libby any harm! I . . .'

'No, I know who you meant to harm, because I can see right through you,' hissed Will furiously. 'Carlotta! Because you're jealous of her. Well, you've gone too far this time, Fern!' He turned abruptly and walked to the door.

'Where are you going?' whispered Fern hoarsely.

'I'm going to ride to St Clare's and see if I can't get Libby out of this mess somehow,' he answered shortly. 'And you're going to have some explaining to do tomorrow morning. Just hope that Mum and Dad don't get to hear about this. Because, if they do, I'll see to it that they find out about your part in it too, you little sneak!'

Turning his back on his cousin, Will slipped silently out of the house and sped towards the stables. Thank goodness Carlotta had shown him how to ride bareback so that he didn't need to waste time saddling a horse! Within seconds he was on his way to St Clare's. He had no idea what he was going to do once he got there, but he just couldn't sit back and do nothing when his sister and Carlotta were in trouble.

It was fortunate for Will that Mam'zelle was delayed on her way to the common-room, which was at the other end of the building. She had walked half-way there when she suddenly remembered that she had left the light on in the head's study and, with an exclamation of annoyance, she retraced her steps. Then she encountered one of the school cats, who did not like being cooped up indoors on a warm night like this. His demands to be let out were loud enough to wake the entire school, so the irate French mistress had to go and open a window for him. All of this gained Will precious minutes.

Leaving his horse at the school gates, Will ran across the lawn. Libby had shown him her common-room at half-term, so he was able to go directly to the right window. The third formers were sitting around sucking chocolates and telling silly jokes that had them all in stitches, when a soft tapping noise came at the window. This stopped their laughter most effectively, Alison clutching at Rachel in terror, while Gladys jumped so violently that she spilt lemonade on her nightie.

'What was that?' asked Isabel, looking scared.

The tapping came again and the girls stared at one another, frightened.

'Perhaps it's a burglar,' suggested Doris in a shaking voice.

'Nonsense!' said the down-to-earth Bobby. 'Burglars don't knock!' And, getting to her feet, she pulled aside the curtain and exclaimed, 'Why, it's your brother, Libby!'

Astonished, Libby went across and pulled open the window. 'Will, what's wrong? Oh, don't say that Mum and Dad have discovered I'm missing!'

Will shook his head and said hastily, 'You have to come with me now, Libby. One of your mistresses knows that there's a feast and she's on her way here.'

There was a collective gasp of horror, voices demanding, 'How could anyone have found out?' And, 'How do you know all this, Will?'

'No time to explain,' he said hastily. 'Libby can tell you everything tomorrow. Come on, sis, out through the window!'

'No,' said Libby stubbornly. 'I've joined in the feast, so if we are to be caught I shall share in the punishment.'

Just then the girls heard the unmistakable sound of footsteps along the corridor – the kind of footsteps made by large, flat shoes. Mam'zelle!

'Libby, this is no time for heroism,' hissed Janet, almost pushing the girl out of the window. 'Any punishment we get will be ten times worse if you're found here as well! For Heaven's sake, go!'

Seeing the sense of this, Libby scrambled hastily on to the window-ledge, jumping down on to the grass just as the door burst open and Mam'zelle stormed in. The brother and sister could hear her scolding angrily as they ran across the grounds.

'Phew, I wouldn't like to be in their shoes!' murmured Will. Then, suddenly, he stopped abruptly, pulling Libby to a halt. 'Carlotta!' he exclaimed. 'I forgot all about her. I didn't see her in the common-room. Where is she?'

'Oh, Carlotta's in the sickbay,' explained Libby. 'She was taken ill this morning, poor thing, and couldn't come to the feast.'

'Well, thank goodness for that!' said Will, beginning to walk on. 'So Fern's nasty little scheme backfired after all.'

'What!' cried Libby, clutching at her brother's arm. 'Do you mean to tell me that Fern was behind this?'

Her voice sounded very loud in the still night and Will

hissed, 'Sh, idiot! You'll bring that fierce French mistress of yours out here and I don't want that.'

'Then tell me,' demanded Libby, lowering her voice. 'Was it Fern?'

'Yes,' said Will, sounding unusually grave. 'She telephoned the school – anonymously, of course – and gave the game away. I heard her moving about, came downstairs to investigate and overhead the whole thing. And didn't I tell her what I thought of her!'

'The mean, deceitful little sneak!' hissed Libby, trembling with anger. 'Your ticking off will be nothing compared to what I intend to say to her when we get home!'

They had reached the gates by this time, and Will patted the horse's neck, saying, 'I wouldn't say anything to her tonight if I were you, otherwise it'll end in a full-scale row and we're likely to wake the parents. Save it for tomorrow. Now come on, climb up behind me and let's go home. I don't know about you, but all this excitement has tired me out.'

Libby felt too blazingly angry at that moment to be tired, her mind working furiously as she mounted the horse. How she was going to control herself and keep from flying at Fern tomorrow, she just didn't know!'

A very angry third form

Mam'zelle was absolutely furious with the third formers, of course, giving them a really dreadful ticking off before escorting them back to their dormitories.

'You are all wicked girls!' she cried. 'Tomorrow you will clear up the common-room after breakfast, then you will go to Miss Theobald.'

'Yes, Mam'zelle,' answered the girls meekly as they got into bed feeling subdued. What a horrid ending to such a wonderful day.

'Now I go,' said Mam'zelle. 'And if I hear one sound from either of these dormitories tonight, you will all do one hour's extra French prep every evening next week.'

The girls would have loved to discuss the extraordinary events of the evening, but they knew Mam'zelle well enough to be certain that she would carry out her threat. Not one of them, even the daring Bobby, had the courage to utter a single word after she had gone.

Next morning, though, they had plenty to say as they tidied up the common-room, removing all traces of the feast. They felt extremely tired, and groaned as they went about their work.

'Thank goodness Libby managed to get away,' said

Hilary. 'If her parents had found out that she had sneaked out there would have been fireworks!'

'And Carlotta is in the clear, too,' remarked Pat. 'At least that's something to be thankful for.'

'Yes, but there are a couple of things that are very puzzling,' said Isabel. 'How did Mam'zelle find out about our feast? And how did Will know that *she* knew, and manage to get here in the nick of time? It's all most mysterious!'

'I daresay that Libby has found out what happened by now,' said Bobby. 'We'll just have to be patient until she comes over.'

At the Oaks, meanwhile, Fern had managed to avoid Libby so far. Last night she had pretended to be asleep when her cousin had returned from the feast, and this morning she had stayed close to her aunt. Now, though, Mr and Mrs Francis had gone out, and Fern could no longer put off the inevitable confrontation.

Libby wasted no time, waiting only until her parents' car had pulled away before going up to her cousin and pushing her roughly. 'What have you got to say for yourself, you horrid little sneak?'

'I'm sorry, Libby,' muttered Fern, hanging her head. 'I didn't mean *you* any harm.'

'No, you meant to harm Carlotta!' said Libby, her lip curling. 'Well, your miserable little plan failed, because Carlotta wasn't at the feast! She was in the sickbay!'

Fern felt sick too when she heard this. She was in disgrace with both of her cousins and it had all been for nothing!

'I can't understand you, Fern!' cried Libby. 'I was at the feast, your own cousin – not to mention Alison, who is supposed to be your friend! Yet you were willing to sacrifice both of us just so that you could get at Carlotta.'

Fern made no attempt to defend herself. There was really nothing she could say. She decided that her best chance of getting round Libby was by being meek and apologetic. Her eyes downcast, she said in a subdued tone, 'You've every right to be angry with me. What will you do now?'

'I shan't do anything,' answered Libby, and a gleam of satisfaction shone in her cousin's eyes. Libby wasn't going to betray her to the others! But Fern had rejoiced too soon, for Libby went on coolly, 'Your punishment must be left to the other third formers – the ones who were caught out and punished themselves, thanks to your mean trick.'

'Libby, you surely don't mean to tell them that it was me who spoilt the feast!' cried Fern, her meek pose forgotten now. 'You can't! I'm your cousin and you ought to be loyal to me, not them!'

'Don't you dare talk to me about loyalty!' growled Libby, sounding so fierce that her cousin shrank back. 'You don't know the meaning of the word! I've thought long and hard about this and I don't see why I should cover up for you. The others have a right to know who was the cause of the trouble they are in, and sending you to Coventry for a time might make you stop and think.'

Looking at the determination in her cousin's face, Fern knew that it was no use trying to make Libby change her mind. But how would she face the others and stand their contempt?

Reading the girl's thoughts, Libby said harshly, 'You can think yourself lucky that it's the weekend and you don't have to face the girls for a couple of days. And don't think of trying to get out of going to school on Monday by pretending to be ill again, or I shall tell Mum everything, even if it means getting into trouble myself. Now I'm going across to St Clare's to find out what happened after Mam'zelle stopped the feast.'

The third formers, a subdued lot that afternoon after a stern talk from Miss Theobald, were pleased to see Libby, for they were longing to know what Will had had to say. They were gathered by the swimming-pool when the girl arrived, calling out, 'Hi, everyone! What happened? Is everyone OK?'

'Miss Theobald says we aren't allowed to leave the grounds for a fortnight,' said Doris mournfully. 'By which time she hopes we will have learnt to behave in a more "mature and responsible manner".'

'Oh, no, that's too bad!' exclaimed Libby. 'It was only thanks to Will that I wasn't caught too.'

'Yes, what happened about that, Libby?' asked Bobby curiously. 'How did Will know that Mam'zelle was going to stop the feast?'

Libby told her, and the third formers listened in gathering wrath.

'The nasty little sneak!'

'How low can you get? She deserves to be sent to Coventry for the rest of the term.'

'She deserves worse than that!' cried Janet. 'If I had her here now, I'd throw her in the swimming-pool!'

Janet felt particularly guilty about the feast going wrong because it was she who had goaded Carlotta into saying that the day girls could come. Libby had escaped being caught by a whisker and if Carlotta hadn't been taken ill, she would certainly have been held responsible. Janet still felt a little resentment towards Carlotta, but coming so close to disaster had made her realize that she didn't want the girl to lose her position because of anything she had done.

'Well, I'll leave the rest of you to discuss what's to be done with Fern,' said Libby. 'I'm going to pop along to the sickbay and see if Matron will let me spend some time with Carlotta.'

'I expect she needs a bit of cheering up,' said Isabel. 'Pat and I went along earlier to give her some birthday cake but she was asleep so we had to leave it with Matron. Do give her our love.'

Carlotta was, in fact, feeling very much better when Libby – after a stern warning from Matron not to stay too long or over-excite the patient – entered the sickbay. 'Oh, how marvellous to see someone other than Matron,' she sighed happily. 'I've been bored to tears all day and just dying to hear about the feast. Do sit down and tell me all about it, Libby. I'll bet it was fantastic. How I wish I had been there!'

'Well, as it turns out, it's a very, good thing that you weren't,' said Libby drily and at once launched into the tale of the spoilt feast and Fern's part in it, Carlotta interrupting with many astonished questions and exclamations. By the end of the story, her dark eyes sparkled angrily and she said in a low, trembling voice, 'So! Fern wanted to hurt me so badly that she was prepared to get the entire form into a row. How she must hate me!'

Carlotta felt hurt as well as angry. This wasn't the first time that she had come up against spite and jealousy, but she had never met anyone who loathed her as intensely and bitterly as Fern did.

Seeing her flushed cheeks, Libby became alarmed and cried, 'I shouldn't have told you yet! What an idiot I am! Matron warned me not to excite you, so I promptly go and do just that. Oh, I could kick myself!'

Seeing that Libby was really worried, Carlotta forced herself to calm down and even managed a smile. 'Don't worry, Libby,' she said. 'I'm not about to have a relapse. In fact, I fully intend to be fit for school on Monday – fighting fit!'

Before she could say any more, Matron came in and shooed Libby away. She was thoughtful as she made her way back to the others. Libby had got to know Carlotta very well and, although she had heard tales of the girl's fiery temper, she had never before seen such a blaze of anger in her eyes. Fern was really going to get it hot on Monday!

But there was no time to brood on that now, for when she returned to the swimming-pool, Rachel called out,

'Right, everyone! Now that Libby's back, how about fitting in another rehearsal?'

The form was divided on this, some girls thinking it an excellent idea, while others called out, 'Oh, no! It's too hot!'

'Well, we could do with something to take our minds off all the nasty things that have been happening lately,' said Rachel with sound good sense. 'And we're going to have some spare time on our hands for the next fortnight as we can't go into town, so I vote we put it to good use. Come on!'

'You know, you're becoming quite a slave driver!' said Janet, half amused and half admiring Rachel's determination as the girls filed indoors.

'I'm a real dragon once I get going,' laughed Rachel. 'Before long you'll be begging Carlotta to come back.'

Of course, Rachel wasn't a slave driver or a dragon. The girls were only too keen to do their best for her, spurred on by her drive and enthusiasm. For a while, the girls were able to forget their woes – and their anger – as they threw themselves whole-heartedly into the rehearsal.

But several of the third formers discussed Fern's behaviour after prep in the common-room.

'She's going to have to be hauled over the coals about this,' said Pat. 'I only hope that Carlotta is back in class on Monday, then she can call a form meeting to decide how to deal with her.'

'I know how I would like to deal with her,' said Bobby menacingly. 'Horrid creature!'

'Yes, but we mustn't put ourselves in the wrong,' pointed out Isabel sensibly. 'Hey, Alison, I hope you're going to back us up on this, and not let Fern charm her way back into your good books!'

'No fear of that, Isabel,' said Alison with unusual firmness. 'She's no friend of mine! And I'm looking forward to seeing that she gets her come-uppance on Monday.'

17

A hard time for Fern

Fern was afraid. She had delayed coming to school that morning until the last possible moment, sidling into the classroom seconds before Miss Adams. It was impossible for the third formers to say anything to her then, but they still made their feelings plain, with hard stares and scornful glances. Fern remembered the day of the auditions, when she had put the stable clock back to make Carlotta late. How she wished that she could *really* turn back time now, and never make that ill-fated telephone call.

At break-time Miss Adams was surprised when Fern, whom she considered spoilt and lazy, offered to stay in and help her tidy out the cupboard in the classroom. But when lunch-time came it was impossible for the girl to avoid the others any longer.

Carlotta, whom Matron had declared well enough to return to class, approached her in the courtyard and said coldly, 'The girls would like you to come to the common-room. There is something we would like to say to you.'

'I . . . I can't come,' stammered Fern. 'I'm busy.'

'No you're not!' cried Libby, coming up at that moment. 'You're just trying to wriggle out of facing us!

You just come along now and don't make us even more ashamed of you than we already are.'

Fern's heart sank. There was nothing for it but to go with the two girls. She felt even more miserable when they entered the common-room and she saw cold unfriendly faces all around her. She glanced at Alison, hoping for a flicker of sympathy, but Alison stared right through her.

Carlotta took the floor. A very angry Carlotta. But she had made up her mind to hold on to her temper and not stamp her foot or fly into a rage, as she would have done a few terms ago. She was head of the form and, as such, would handle this affair with the dignity her position demanded. Indeed, her demeanour surprised and very much impressed the others. 'You know why you are here, Fern,' she began, looking contemptuously at the girl. 'You played a very mean, spiteful trick on the girls the other night and must be punished for it.'

Although she felt frightened, Carlotta's scornful tone stung Fern and she retorted, 'I won't be punished by *you*! You weren't even at the feast, so this has nothing to do with you!'

'Oh, yes it does!' said Pat angrily. 'We all know that you planned the whole thing to get at Carlotta because you're jealous of her!'

'Jealous of *her*?' sneered Fern, with an incredulous laugh. 'What nonsense! Carlotta is nothing but a common, low-down . . .' But she was not allowed to continue, a chorus of angry voices shouting her down.

'You're the one who's low down! Rotten sneak!'

'Carlotta is worth a dozen of you!'

Carlotta herself gave a scornful laugh. Fern's insults meant nothing to her at all. 'You are being punished by the whole of the form, not just me,' she told the girl harshly. 'We've all talked about this and agreed what we have to do. As from now, you are in Coventry, Fern. None of us wishes to speak to you or have anything to do with you. We don't want you coming here at weekends or joining in any of our after-school activities. Whether we change our minds nearer the end of term depends upon how well you learn your lesson and whether or not you are truly sorry.'

That was the beginning of a horrid time for Fern. Never in her pampered life had she been treated like this. It was very hard to be met with silence and blank stares everywhere she went, just dreadful to have no one to chatter and laugh with. Things were just as bad at home, too, with both Libby and Will against her. In fact the only people who ever gave her a kind word were Aunt Polly and Uncle Tom. Once she bumped into Alison in the corridor. She was alone and Fern, desperate for a smile or a friendly word, approached her.

'Alison, I'm sorry!' she said, making her eyes wide and trying her best to sound sincere. 'I know it was a dreadful thing to do, and I just wish I could put things right between us.'

Carlotta and Rachel came round the corner, just in time to hear the end of this plea, and Alison turned to them, saying with a puzzled look, 'Did either of you two hear a noise just then?'

Rachel shook her head. 'Not a thing.'

'Me neither,' said Carlotta. 'Must have been the wind!'

And with that the three girls walked away, leaving Fern to stare after them, torn between despair and anger. Alison *would* have made it up with her, Fern was quite convinced, if only that horrible Carlotta and that awful Rachel hadn't turned up. It was *their* fault! In fact, they were to blame for everything bad that had happened to her since coming to this dreadful school! Foolish, jealous Fern couldn't see that she was her own worst enemy.

There was now just over a week left until the end of term and preparations for the play were in full swing. The girls knew their parts off by heart, the costumes were almost finished and handwritten invitations had been sent out to all the parents of the third formers. Then a series of mishaps occurred which put the future of the play in jeopardy.

First, Doris caught the same flu bug which had laid Carlotta low. Unfortunately, in her case, it led to a very bad throat infection which left her barely able to croak. Matron insisted that she rest her voice completely and did not attempt to speak for several days, which meant, of course, that she was unable to rehearse.

'This is a disaster!' wailed Rachel in despair. 'Doris is one of our stars and quite irreplaceable.'

'Well, if she takes Matron's advice and rests her voice, she may not need to be replaced,' pointed out Hilary with her customary common sense. 'Do try not to get too down in the dumps, Rachel, when there may not be any need.'

Isabel stood in for Doris during rehearsals, but she lacked Doris's comic touch and felt very second-best, as she said to her twin. Isabel, almost more than Rachel, hoped devoutly that Doris would be all right on the night.

Then another blow fell. The girls had gratefully accepted a generous offer from the second formers to paint some scenery for the play. The second did a marvellous job and when they had finished, Rachel said, 'Thank you all so much! You really have been a big help.'

'Just make sure that we get good seats on the night, Rachel,' laughed Grace, head of the second form. 'Now we really ought to put this somewhere safe to dry.'

'Stand it outside against the garden wall,' suggested Bobby. 'It will dry beautifully over night.'

Alas, in the early hours of the following morning there was an unexpected downpour, so that the scenery was quite ruined. The third formers were distraught.

'We'll never have time to paint it again,' groaned Pat.

'We have to find time!' said Rachel with determination, though inwardly she felt dismayed. She might have known that everything had been going too smoothly! And now it all seemed to be falling apart.

'I wonder what next?' said Mirabel. 'Things like this always seem to happen in threes.'

'Thanks for that optimistic thought, Mirabel,' said Janet drily.

'Oh, that's nonsense anyway,' said the down-to-earth

Pat. 'Surely nothing else terrible can happen?'

But, sadly, Mirabel was proved right. Something terrible did happen – and to her!

Mirabel, a very fine tennis player, was in a school match that weekend. The entire third form turned out to watch her, their cheers and applause filling the air every time she scored a point. Her opponent was an excellent player too, and the match a close one. In the final set, Mirabel's opponent made a magnificent serve, sending the ball soaring over her head. Mirabel, though, believed in fighting for every point, however hopeless it seemed, and leapt backwards, her racket stretched upwards. Suddenly she stumbled and fell awkwardly, letting out a cry of pain.

'Oh, no, I don't like the sound of that!' said Janet.

'She'll be all right,' said Rachel, with more confidence than she felt. 'Just a nasty twist, I expect.'

'Mirabel wouldn't squeal if she had just twisted her ankle,' said a grave Gladys, who knew her friend well. 'Something is badly wrong.'

Indeed it was. Mirabel had a very nasty sprain and would have to rest her foot completely for a couple of days. Even then it would be a while before she could put her weight on it completely. Naturally, everyone's first concern was for Mirabel, who really was in quite a lot of pain. But once the third formers were satisfied that no lasting damage had been done, their thoughts turned to the play.

'I've just had the most awful thought!' exclaimed Janet in the common-room that evening. 'Mirabel can't possibly play the part of Lord Derwent if she can't walk properly! It's such an active role.'

As Lady Dorinda's clumsy husband, Mirabel had to stumble around the stage, tripping over, bumping into furniture and knocking things down. Her ankle would never stand the strain. Seeing the look of despair on Rachel's face as the realization of this sank in, Alison said hastily, 'Perhaps you can rewrite Mirabel's scenes so that she can do them sitting down.'

'Impossible!' sighed Rachel, her expression bleak. 'She can't create all the chaos that Lord Derwent is supposed to by sitting in a chair throughout. It's almost as though there's a jinx on the play.'

Fern, although the others would not speak to her, kept her ears open and heard all about the so-called jinx. She also overheard Miss Adams say to Miss Walker, the art mistress, 'I feel so sorry for them! They have all worked terribly hard. But if one more thing goes wrong, I really think that will mean the end of the third's play.'

Fern thought about this long and hard. Empty headed she might be in many ways, but the girl could be cunning when she wanted something badly. And Fern wanted nothing more than to hurt Carlotta and Rachel. If she could spoil Rachel's play and make it look as though Carlotta was responsible, she would have a fine revenge on both of them. Suddenly everything became clear to Fern. She knew exactly what she had to do!

18

Fern is foolish

Sunday was yet another gloriously sunny day, and the afternoon saw all the girls playing tennis or splashing about in the swimming-pool. It was an easy matter for Fern to slip unseen into the school. She went first to Carlotta's dormitory and, going to the girl's locker, removed a pair of pearl-handled embroidery scissors. Carlotta did not use these very often, for needlework was not one of her talents, but Fern – along with the rest of the form – knew that she treasured them because they had belonged to her mother.

The dainty scissors in her pocket, Fern slipped stealthily downstairs and made her way to the storeroom behind the hall where the costumes for the play were neatly hung up. There was the elegant dress Gladys was to wear as Lady Dorinda, a man's suit for Mirabel and Doris's policeman's uniform. A real feeling of spite welling up in her, Fern removed the scissors from her pocket and got to work, slitting seams, removing buttons and making long slashes in the material. Within a short time, the costumes were ruined. Surveying her handiwork gleefully, Fern dropped Carlotta's scissors on the floor and slipped away.

How she rejoiced as she made her way home, thinking

of what would happen when the third formers discovered their spoilt costumes and saw Carlotta's scissors nearby. With one blow she had hit back at both her enemies. Rachel would be devastated. And Carlotta would know what it was like to be shunned, for the others would certainly want no more to do with her. But Fern's euphoric mood was short lived. The first thing she saw on returning home were Libby, Will and Carlotta, chatting together companionably as they led their horses into the paddock. None of them appeared to have noticed her slip away, and not one of them glanced round now as she returned. Carlotta said something in her funny little up-and-down voice, which made the others shout with laughter, and Fern felt certain that the remark had been about her. Bitterness welled up in her as she watched the three mount. Carlotta cantered off at once, Will close behind as he called out, 'Show us that trick you did the other day, Carlotta! It was just great.' Even Fern had to admit, grudgingly, that Carlotta made a charming picture on horseback, her lightly tanned cheeks glowing and her eyes sparkling with pleasure. Fern remembered all the times over the years that Will had offered to teach her to ride but she had always refused. If only she had accepted his offer, she might be riding round the paddock now, and her cousin's words of praise would be for her, instead of that hateful Carlotta. The three riders turned their horses and trotted past the gate where Fern was standing. They did not look at her, or acknowledge her presence in any way.

Suddenly Fern felt quite unable to bear being ignored any longer. Anger boiled inside her, so fierce that it made her tremble, taking hold of her. She would *make* her cousins notice her – and Fern knew exactly the way to do it! Anger lending her courage, she marched to the stables and unbolted one of the doors. There stood the big black horse that Carlotta sometimes rode. And anything Carlotta could do, Fern could do. After all, the girl was no bigger or stronger than she. Hesitantly she reached out and stroked the horse's velvety nose, feeling reassured when he whinnied softly and gently nudged her shoulder.

Rocky had calmed down a great deal over the last few weeks and now loved to be petted by almost anyone. However there were still only two people he would allow on his back – Will or Carlotta. Fern, who had never taken any interest in the 'horse talk' her cousins were so fond of, didn't know this. Doubtfully she looked at the bewildering array of tack that hung from the stable wall and abandoned the idea of trying to saddle the horse. She simply didn't have the first idea how to go about it and would only waste time. She had seen Carlotta ride bareback dozens of times, so it couldn't be that difficult. Standing on an upturned bucket and clutching the horse's mane, Fern managed to hoist herself up on to the horse's back. Once there, she didn't feel quite so confident. The ground seemed an awfully long way down, and when Rocky made even the tiniest movement she felt that she would fall off. Rocky was really behaving in an unusually docile manner, and when Fern made the same clicking noise with her tongue that she had heard the others do, he walked forward obediently. That was when the girl realized that she had bitten off more than she could chew. She began to slide sideways and grabbed hard at the horse's mane, giving a frightened little squeal which Rocky didn't like at all! Suddenly he seemed to realize that the person on his back wasn't his beloved Carlotta or his adored Will, but a stranger, and his aim was to unseat her at all costs. He bucked sharply and Fern squealed again but hung on for dear life, her fingers firmly entwined in the horse's mane. That was when Rocky decided to show her who was boss and, tossing his black head with an air of contempt, cantered through the stable yard, past the paddock where the others were riding, and into an open field, Fern shrieking wildly all the time. She achieved her object, however – the others took notice, all right! Libby pulled her horse up sharply, her cheeks turning white.

'Oh, my goodness!' she gasped. 'Rocky's bolted with Fern. What on earth is she doing on his back anyway?'

'Never mind that now,' said Will grimly. 'The important thing is to get her off, the little idiot! Carlotta, come with me and we'll try to pull him up. Libby, you stay here. We may need you to call for an ambulance!'

Libby turned paler still at this, her eyes wide and staring, as Rocky became a black dot in the distance.

Carlotta looked worried too as she urged her mount forward and sent him leaping over the fence that divided the paddock from the field. 'Whatever possessed her to mount Rocky?' she cried over her shoulder to Will as he caught up.

'Oh, Fern wouldn't have known that he was dangerous,' answered Will. 'She knows nothing about the horses, and one is just like another to her.'

Neither of them questioned why Fern had found it necessary to take a horse at all, for they knew – she was absolutely desperate for attention.

'We're gaining on them!' called Carlotta. 'Come on, Silver! Oh, my word, that was close!'

This last remark came as Rocky stumbled and Fern was jolted so badly that she almost lost her grip. The shock of losing his footing seemed to confuse Rocky and he circled round, heading back towards the paddock. Carlotta seized the opportunity, turning Silver deftly and edging closer and closer until the two horses were almost neck and neck.

'Hello, Rocky,' she crooned softly.

The horse recognized her voice at once and slowed, turning his head and whinnying in pleasure. Fern, by this time, was a crumpled, sobbing heap, her knuckles white from the effort of holding on, and it was evident that she could not do so for much longer. Carlotta edged forward, so that she was almost standing in the stirrups, and leant across to pat Rocky's neck. Then she tugged gently on his mane, he stopped abruptly and Fern half fell and half slid to the ground.

It was unfortunate that, as this drama was taking place, Mr and Mrs Francis, who had been out, drove into the stable yard. Libby ran to them as soon as they got out of the car and told them quickly what had happened. Both of them were horrified, running to the gate and watching in terror as Fern landed on the ground. Mrs Francis did not realize that Carlotta had the situation under control and ran towards her niece.

'It's all right!' called Carlotta, who had dismounted and was bending to help Fern up. But Mrs Francis was so frantic with worry that she did not hear, moving forward and crying sharply, 'Fern! Oh, my goodness! Are you all right?'

Rocky, disliking the sudden noise and flurry of movement, reared up and flailed his hooves. One of them struck Carlotta on the back of the head and she keeled over, unconscious.

'Oh, no!' cried Libby, tears springing to her eyes. 'Carlotta!'

While these dramatic events were unfolding, the third formers were preparing to go in to tea at St Clare's.

'Half a minute!' said Rachel. 'I've just remembered that I promised to take Gladys's dress to Miss Stratton this afternoon for a small alteration. I'll just fetch it.'

Miss Stratton was the needlework mistress, whose help with the costumes had been quite invaluable.

'All right, but hurry up,' said Janet.

The others waited outside while Rachel went into the little storeroom. She was gone a long time and when she emerged she looked rather pale and upset.

'You've been ages!' complained Bobby. 'And you still haven't got Gladys's dress, goof! Hey, whatever's up? You look awfully strange.'

'Come with me,' said Rachel in a rather strangled voice. 'There's something I think all of you ought to see.'

Puzzled, the girls followed her, gasping in horror when they saw the ruined costumes.

'They're all spoilt!' cried Pat, shocked. 'Whatever can have happened to them?'

'Not what. Who?' said Hilary coming forward to examine them. 'They have been cut deliberately.'

'But who could have done such a dreadful thing?' gasped Isabel in dismay.

Janet's sharp eyes had spotted the scissors on the floor and she picked them up, holding them out in answer. Every girl recognized them at once.

'Carlotta's!' exclaimed Alison. 'No, I don't believe it! She would never do such a thing.'

'I agree,' said Pat stoutly. 'Why, what possible reason could she have?'

'Perhaps she felt more angry than she let on about being replaced as director,' suggested Janet coolly.

'No!' protested Isabel. 'When Carlotta feels angry she lets people know about it! This certainly isn't her work.'

'Well, they're certainly her scissors,' said Hilary uncomfortably. 'But everyone knows where she keeps them and any one of us could have slipped into the dormitory and taken them. I certainly wouldn't be prepared to accuse her without much stronger proof than this.'

Suddenly the door opened and Miss Theobald entered looking unusually grave. The girls at once fell silent and realized that they were late for tea. In fact, they had forgotten all about it thanks to this act of sabotage. But it seemed that Miss Theobald had not come to give them a telling off. She was here on a much more serious matter indeed.

Bad news - and good news

'I am sorry to have to tell you all that there has been an accident at the Oaks, involving Carlotta and Fern,' said the head seriously.

The girls stared at her in silent horror for a moment, then everyone spoke at once.

'Are they all right?'

'What kind of accident?'

'Miss Theobald, Carlotta isn't badly hurt, is she? What happened?'

'I am afraid that I don't have any details at the moment,' said Miss Theobald. 'I am going to the hospital now, to meet Mr and Mrs Francis and find out what the situation is.'

The girls felt badly shaken when they heard this. Fern and Carlotta must be in a bad way if they were in hospital.

'Libby is in the common-room,' the head went on. 'Apparently she witnessed the accident and is, naturally, extremely shocked and upset. Her parents thought it best to leave her among friends and I have assured them that you will take good care of her.'

'You can rely on us, Miss Theobald,' said Hilary seriously. 'Come on, girls, let's go and cheer Libby up a bit.'

None of the girls felt at all like tea now, their appetites completely destroyed by this piece of shocking news. Libby was huddled on a sofa in the common-room, looking very pale and trembling from head to foot. At once, Pat went across and took her hand, saying kindly, 'Poor Libby! You really have had a shock.'

'Do you want to tell us what happened?' asked Isabel gently.

Her voice quivering, and close to tears at times, Libby told the whole story.

'Poor Carlotta!' exclaimed Gladys. 'She rescued Fern so bravely, only to be injured herself! How is Fern, by the way?'

Libby gave a bitter laugh. 'Absolutely fine, apart from a few bruises. She's gone to hospital in the car with my parents. Mum insisted that the doctor check her over, just to be on the safe side, but I think she's perfectly all right. It's Carlotta I'm worried about. She had to be taken by ambulance, and my brother Will went along with her. He said that it was so that she would see a familiar face if she came round on the journey, but I think he just wanted a ride in an ambulance!' Again Libby laughed, but it broke in the middle and she began to sob. 'Carlotta looked so white and still! Oh, I do hope that she'll be all right.'

'Of course she will,' said Pat, sounding more confident than she felt.

'This is just terrible!' said Rachel, looking very upset. 'And now I find it harder than ever to believe that Carlotta was to blame for destroying our costumes. A girl with enough courage and nerve to stop a runaway horse couldn't possibly be guilty of that kind of mean-spirited behaviour. Not that I've ever considered Carlotta mean spirited. Quite the reverse, in fact!'

'Whatever are you talking about?' asked Libby, distracted from her worries for a moment.

The third formers told her about the costumes, and the girl exclaimed hotly, 'Of course Carlotta wouldn't do such a thing! But I think I know who would!'

'Who?' asked Alison, her blue eyes wide.

'Isn't it obvious?' said Libby scornfully. 'The same person who has been behind all the upsets in the third form this term!'

'Fern!' cried everyone.

'Yes, Fern,' said Libby grimly. 'And now that I come to think of it, she disappeared for a while this afternoon. Quite long enough for her to come over here and carry out her spiteful little plan.'

'I expect it seemed a marvellous opportunity to get back at Carlotta and me,' said Rachel thoughtfully.

'What a despicable trick!' said Bobby. 'To make it look as though Carlotta was to blame! And how ironic that Carlotta should save Fern after she had done such a mean thing to her.'

'That girl needs a thorough shaking up!' said Mirabel.

'I think she's had one,' said Libby. 'She really was terribly shocked and upset when Carlotta was hurt. I just hope that she's learnt something from all this.'

'And I just hope that Miss Theobald has good news for us when she comes back,' said Pat.

The others echoed this heartily as they settled down for a long wait. Never had time passed so slowly as all the girls prayed silently for their friend. Suddenly the ruined costumes, even the play itself, didn't seem important. All that mattered was that Carlotta should get better.

It was after seven o'clock when Miss Theobald, accompanied by Libby's mother, returned to St Clare's, and it was obvious from their anxious expressions that the news was not good. The girls felt their hearts sinking.

'Carlotta has still not regained consciousness,' said Miss Theobald heavily. 'I have telephoned her father and he is on his way to the hospital now. I'm afraid all that we can do is wait.'

One or two of the girls looked close to tears and Mrs Francis said gently, 'She is in the best possible hands. We must all try to be strong. Come on now, Libby. You must be exhausted. Let's get you home.'

'Oh, Mum, no!' protested Libby. 'I can't! I just can't face Fern after what she's done!'

'Why, Libby!' cried her mother in astonishment. 'I know it was very naughty and thoughtless of Fern to ride Rocky, but she meant no harm.'

'It isn't only that, Mum,' said Libby. 'Fern isn't just thoughtless – she's spiteful and cunning. It was she who sneaked to Mam'zelle about the third's feast, and now she has deliberately ruined our costumes for the play and tried to blame it on Carlotta. I tell you, she's bad!'

The two grown-ups looked at one another in amazement. There was an awful lot here that needed looking into, but now was not the time.

'We would be happy to offer Libby a bed here for the night,' said the head to Mrs Francis. Lowering her voice, she added, 'Perhaps you could have a talk with Fern in the morning, when she has calmed down a little, and let me know the outcome?'

'Yes, of course,' said Libby's mother, looking and sounding extremely worried. She had always been aware of Fern's jealous streak, but the things that Libby had accused her of were really dreadful.

'You don't mind me staying, do you?' said Libby to the others, once the grown-ups had left. 'But the thought of sharing a room with Fern is just too much to bear.'

'Of course we don't mind!' said Hilary warmly. 'Oh, you don't have any night things! Never mind, I'll lend you a nightie.'

'And I've a spare toothbrush you can have,' put in Isabel.

'How about getting some fresh air before bedtime?' suggested Bobby. 'It might tire us out a bit – I think we're all going to find it hard to sleep with this on our minds.'

'Good idea,' said Mirabel, standing up carefully and trying to keep the weight off her injured ankle. 'But I'm afraid I'll have to lean on you, Gladys.'

One girl had taken the news of Carlotta's accident particularly badly. Janet. Unusually for her, she had remained silent while the others talked. She did not follow them outside now, but remained behind in the silent and deserted common-room, feeling as though the weight of the world was on her shoulders. Only now, with Carlotta desperately ill, did Janet realize just how fond of the girl she was, her resentment and bitterness of the last few weeks disappearing and leaving behind only remorse. Every bit as brave in her own way as Carlotta, Janet faced up honestly to the petty way she had been behaving. Even when the damaged costumes had been discovered, Janet had been unable to stop herself making a snide remark about Carlotta, although she had known, in her heart, that the girl was not capable of such spitefulness. No, Carlotta was not a spiteful person. Nor was she, Janet, as a rule. But envy had made her behave like one. It was a sobering and unpleasant thought.

A movement by the door caught her eye and she looked up to see Mam'zelle standing there.

'I was looking for Miss Adams and thought that she might be here,' said the French mistress. 'But I see it is not so.'

She looked closely at Janet and, seeing her bleak expression, came into the room, saying anxiously, 'What is the matter, *ma chère*? You look very – how is it? – down in the face.'

'You mean down in the mouth, Mam'zelle,' said Janet, with the ghost of her usual smile. 'Yes, I was just thinking about Carlotta.'

'Ah, yes!' The corners of Mam'zelle's mouth turned down, her sloe-black eyes became sombre. 'The poor Carlotta! But she will be all right. I feel it here!' She put a hand to her heart. 'What a dreadful end to her term as head girl. I hope that you will have a better time when it is your turn next term, *ma petite*!'

Janet stared at Mam'zelle and said, 'Why, whatever do you mean?'

Mam'zelle looked sheepish suddenly and cried, '*Oh, là là!* Now I have let the cat out of his sack and put him among the sparrows!'

'You mean, let the cat out of the bag and . . . oh, never mind, Mam'zelle. But what *do* you mean?'

Mam'zelle sighed and shrugged expressively. 'I may as well tell you now. But, please, Janet, it must be a secret between the two of us for now, *oui*?'

'*Oui*,' agreed Janet at once, bursting with curiosity.

Mam'zelle told her of the head's decision that the two girls take turns at being head girl. 'So you see,' she finished. 'You are to be head of the form next term.'

Janet listened with mixed feelings. At any other time she would have been thrilled by this news. But now, knowing that her resentment of Carlotta had been for nothing, she could not find it in herself to feel happy.

'We must keep up our chins,' declared Mam'zelle stoutly, patting Janet's cheek. 'And pray for the dear Carlotta. Ah, Miss Theobald told me all about Fern and her wickedness. To think that she is responsible for all this. Truly, jealousy is a terrible thing!'

Yes, jealousy *is* terrible, agreed Janet silently. And, in her own way, she was every bit as bad as Fern, for she had allowed it to eat away at her. But Janet was a strong character and had learnt a valuable lesson. Never again, she vowed, would she allow jealousy to take control of her. She would conquer it, and become a better person as a result. And once Carlotta was well, she would make things up to her in every way she could.

As Janet was thinking these thoughts, Bobby suddenly burst into the room, crying, 'Janet, there you are! Why didn't you come outside? Oh, excuse me, Mam'zelle! The thing is, we've just seen Miss Theobald and she's had the most marvellous news! The hospital telephoned her to say that Carlotta has come round and she's going to be all right. Isn't that wonderful?'

A lump suddenly formed in Janet's throat and she said huskily, 'I'll say! The best news in the world!'

20

Things are sorted out

The third formers were all thrilled at the news of Carlotta's recovery, and found it hard to contain their high spirits the next day. Jennifer Mills, the games captain, was almost knocked off her feet by the twins as they ran helter-skelter along the corridor, and she called out sternly, 'Hey, you kids! Watch where you're going, can't you?'

'Sorry, Jenny,' apologized Pat meekly. 'We're just so delighted about Carlotta that we can't seem to keep still.'

'Yes, I heard about that,' said Jenny, her face softening. 'I'm pleased that everything's turned out all right. She's a good kid. Now buzz off, you two and, for Heaven's sake, *walk*!'

The mistresses were very pleased too, for Carlotta was popular with all of them.

'It's extremely good news,' agreed Miss Adams, after the class had spent the first five minutes of their geography lesson that afternoon discussing their friend's recovery. 'But now we really must get on with some work! The head is coming in later to speak to you all, so we will lose quite enough of our lesson as it is.'

'I wonder what Miss Theobald wants to speak to us about?' said Hilary curiously.

'No doubt we will find out in good time,' answered the mistress firmly. 'Now, open your books at page twenty-seven, please.'

The head came into the classroom half-way through the lesson and went across to say something in a low voice to Miss Adams, while the girls got politely to their feet.

'You may sit down,' Miss Theobald said. 'Well, girls, I have some news for you. Mrs Francis came to see me this morning and informed me that Fern has owned up to damaging your costumes, among other things.'

There were several angry murmurs at this and Miss Theobald held up her hand for silence.

'Mrs Francis also told me that she had received a letter from Fern's parents this morning, and that they are returning to England at the weekend. This means that she will be going to live with them, and both her aunt and I agreed that it would be in everyone's best interests if she did not return to St Clare's in the meantime. You have seen the last of her.'

The third formers were glad to hear it. Bobby muttered to Janet, 'Good riddance!'

'I am assured that she feels extremely remorseful about Carlotta's accident,' went on the head. 'We must hope that she will learn from this experience and never be quite so foolish again.'

The third weren't really interested in what happened to Fern, so long as they didn't have to put up with her any longer. They were pleased when Miss Theobald moved on to the subject of Carlotta.

'I visited her in hospital earlier,' she said. 'And I am pleased to report that she is very much better and some of you will be able to visit her tomorrow. Carlotta will be in hospital for several more days, as she needs to rest, but she asked me to tell you all that she is quite determined to be back at school in time for the play.' Miss Theobald's serene face looked grave all of a sudden. 'Naturally I did not tell her about this latest set-back and that the future of the play was looking doubtful, as I felt it would upset her too much.'

'Of course,' said Hilary. 'Thank you for telling us all this, Miss Theobald.'

'Well, I will leave you to get on with your lesson now,' said the head. 'Thank you, Miss Adams.'

'Girls!' cried Janet as the door closed behind Miss Theobald. 'We just *have* to make sure that the play goes ahead somehow! We owe it to Carlotta.'

'I don't see how,' said Isabel gloomily. 'We've no scenery, no costumes, Mirabel can barely walk and Doris can't speak!'

'Oh, yes I can!' piped up Doris, sounding a little husky. 'Matron gave me the all-clear earlier today.'

'Oh, that's wonderful!' exclaimed Pat. 'At least that's one thing we don't have to worry about.'

'Yes,' said Janet thoughtfully. 'Now, if only we can do something about the scenery and . . .'

'Ahem!' broke in Miss Adams, turning a stern look on the class. 'I am delighted that Doris has regained her voice. I am thrilled that you are all so committed to the play. And

I will be positively ecstatic if you can just show a *little* interest in your geography!' After that no one dared mention the play again, but Janet – although she bent her head studiously over her books – did not put it out of her mind. She had a most determined streak in her nature once she set her mind to something, and she intended to see that, one way or another, the third would perform their play.

When afternoon school was over, Rachel said dismally, 'We're meant to be having a rehearsal now, but I don't suppose there's much point.'

'The show must go on!' declared Janet. 'Isn't that what you theatrical folk say?'

'Yes,' laughed Rachel. 'But we're going to have our work cut out, with only a few days left to the end of term. We need a miracle!'

'Well, perhaps we'll have one,' said Janet cryptically. 'Go on with the rehearsal, Rachel, and I'll be back shortly.'

With that she sped away, leaving Rachel to stare after her in surprise. The rehearsal was not a great success at first, for most of the girls felt that they were wasting their time and went through their performances rather woodenly. Then Janet returned, grinning from ear to ear, and Isabel called out from the stage, 'Wow, what's happened to you? You look like a Cheshire cat!'

'Girls,' announced Janet triumphantly. 'The play is saved.'

'So you did work a miracle after all,' said Rachel. 'But how?'

The others demanded to know as well, climbing down

from the stage and crowding round Janet excitedly.

'Well,' she explained. 'I simply asked Miss Walker if it would be possible for all her classes to work on our scenery over the next few days. She's very fond of Carlotta, you know, and agreed at once. Then I took our costumes to Miss Stratton and she thinks that they can be patched up. She pointed out that the audience won't be able to see them close up, so it won't matter too much if the repairs are a bit rough and ready.'

'Fantastic!' cried Pat. 'Well done, Janet. You've really saved the day!'

'But there's one more thing,' said Rachel, frowning. 'And that's Mirabel's part. It's far too late to expect someone else to learn it, yet she can't possibly stand for all that time. I really don't see a way out.'

The solution came from an unexpected source. Alison, who had been listening thoughtfully, piped up, 'I've an idea. You know Matron keeps a couple of wheelchairs in the sickbay? Well, I'm sure she would let us borrow one, then Mirabel would be able to sit down during the play yet still move about the stage, bump into everything, knock tables over and . . .' she broke off suddenly, aware that everyone was staring at her, and turned red. 'Oh, well,' she mumbled. 'Perhaps it wasn't such a good idea, after all.'

'No, it's not a good idea,' said Rachel. 'It's a *brilliant* one! Alison, I could hug you! And next time anyone calls you a feather-head, they'll have me to answer to!'

'And the rest of us!' called out the others. 'Well done, Alison.'

'Come on, then!' Rachel clapped her hands together. 'Why are you all standing around here when you should be on stage? Pat, you're not in this scene, so would you be an angel and pop along to Matron for the wheelchair? The rest of you, places, please!'

The third formers all made time to visit Carlotta over the next three days, and Janet was one of the first. She took with her a huge bar of chocolate and a book she knew Carlotta wanted to read. 'How are you?' she asked gently.

'Oh, miles better,' said Carlotta, who certainly didn't look any the worse for her adventure. 'I seem to have spent most of this term in bed, what with the flu, and now this. I just can't wait to get back to school. Oh, are those for me? How lovely! Sit down and tell me all the news.'

Janet pulled up a chair and began to talk. As the play had been saved, she felt that it was all right to tell Carlotta about Fern and the costumes.

'So,' said Carlotta at last. 'Fern won't be returning to St Clare's. Well, I can't say that I'm sorry. Having so much jealousy directed at you is pretty horrible, you know.'

'I can imagine,' said Janet gravely. 'And you've had a double dose of it – from Fern and from me.'

'*You*, jealous of me?' said Carlotta incredulously. 'Is that the reason you've been so off-ish with me all term? But Janet, *why*?'

'Because you were made head girl,' answered Janet in a small voice. 'I had got it into my mind that I ought to be head of the form, and I felt absolutely *green* when you were chosen!'

'Oh, Janet, if only you had told me!' groaned Carlotta. 'I just couldn't imagine what I had done to offend you.'

'You hadn't done anything,' said Janet. 'It was my own stupid pig-headedness that was to blame. I feel pretty mean about it now, though, especially since Mam'zelle let it slip that I'm to be head girl next term.'

'Really?' exclaimed Carlotta. 'Oh, Janet, I am pleased for you. I'll back you up all the way, you can be sure.'

'I know that you will,' said Janet with unusual humility. 'And it's more than I deserve after the way I've behaved this term.'

'Oh, nonsense!' said Carlotta. 'Now what say we put all this behind us and start afresh next term. And my behaviour hasn't been all that it could be, you know. I've had a lot of time to think while I've been lying here, and I realize that I didn't face up to my responsibilities very well.' Carlotta gave a grimace. 'I got too wrapped up in my friendship with Libby and my horse riding and didn't take as much interest in the affairs of the third as I should have. Well, Libby is leaving at the end of term, so I shall be able to settle down and become a proper member of the form again.'

'Oh, yes, I'd forgotten that Libby was off to America!' exclaimed Janet. 'You'll miss her, won't you? Not to mention the horses!'

'Yes, though I shall still go to the stables and ride with Will from time to time,' answered Carlotta. 'But I shan't be spending so much time over there next term. Instead I shall be with my *old* friends. I've learnt a lesson this term as well, Janet.'

21

A marvellous play

Alison was feeling a little unhappy. Rachel was so busy with last-minute preparations for the play that she seemed to have very little time for her friend. There also seemed to be something guarded and off-hand in her manner these days, and Alison was puzzled and rather hurt by it.

The twins noticed that their cousin looked down in the dumps and wondered why, Pat asking, 'Anything wrong, Alison? You're going round looking like a wet weekend just lately.'

'Yes, do cheer up!' said Isabel. 'We've got such an exciting time ahead of us. The play tomorrow night, then school holidays! Lovely!'

Alison sighed. 'I just can't seem to work up much enthusiasm for anything at the moment. Rachel's being so cold and stand-offish and I can't think why.'

'Rachel's just very tied up with the play right now,' said Pat. 'She'll be her normal self once it's over.'

'That's right,' agreed Isabel. 'We're all feeling pretty nervous about it, wanting to get everything just right, and it must be a hundred times worse for Rachel because it's all in her hands, so to speak.'

Alison so much wanted to believe the twins, who both

had a great deal of common sense. Their cousin didn't have quite so much, but she did feel things deeply – and her feelings still kept on telling her that something wasn't right. But she had to put it to the back of her mind for now as there was so much going on.

The first thing was that Carlotta arrived back at school while the third formers were sitting down to lunch. She slipped in quietly and the first the girls knew of her presence was when they heard her laughing voice saying, 'I hope you've left some for me.'

Then what a hubbub there was, girls scrambling out of their seats to greet Carlotta noisily, even Miss Adams patted the girl on the shoulder and exclaimed that she was happy to see her back. Mam'zelle went a step further, bustling over from her table to envelop Carlotta in a great hug.

'Ah, *ma chère* Carlotta!' she cried, her dark eyes suspiciously moist. 'How good it is that you are well again!'

'Thanks, Mam'zelle,' said Carlotta with a grin. 'It's great to be back.'

'Just in time for dress rehearsal, too,' said Libby, moving up to make room for her friend. 'I hope you've been practising your lines while you've been in hospital, Carlotta.'

'The nurses were sick and tired of hearing me repeat it,' laughed Carlotta. 'And I can't wait for dress rehearsal.'

Dress rehearsal was, in fact, a disaster. Gladys, most unusually for her, was a bundle of nerves and couldn't stop shaking during the entire thing. Bobby tripped as she made her entrance, almost knocking over Pat and sending the others into fits of giggles so that the rehearsal was held up for five minutes while the third formers laughed themselves silly. Then Hilary seemed to forget her lines completely. Rachel, rather to the surprise of the others, wasn't at all put out by this and seemed quite cheerful.

'It's an old theatre superstition,' she explained. 'A good dress rehearsal means that the actual performance will be a disaster – and vice versa.'

'Well, if that's true, we ought to be a roaring success tomorrow night,' laughed Doris.

'We will be!' said Rachel confidently. 'I just know it.'

And Rachel was right! All seemed chaos backstage, with everyone milling about, getting changed and putting their make-up on. The noise was terrific!

'Gladys, do you *really* want to put blue greasepaint on your lips?' called Janet. 'I'm sure you'll find this red one much more suitable.'

'Oh, I'm so nervous I hardly know what I'm doing!' exclaimed Gladys, taking the stick from Janet.

'You'll be all right once the lights go down and you're centre stage,' said Mirabel. 'Then you'll just get right into character and forget everything else.'

'Miss Stratton has done a terrific job with these costumes,' said Doris, donning her policeman's tunic.

'Yes, and Miss Walker's classes have done wonders with the scenery,' said Hilary. 'Whatever would we have done without their help?'

'Looks as if we've got a full house,' said Bobby, peering through the curtains. 'I can see my parents – and yours, Alison. They're right at the front.'

'Oh!' wailed Alison nervously, dropping the pins with which she had been putting up her hair, and scattering them all over the floor. 'I wish you hadn't told me that, Bobby! Now I just *know* I shall fluff my lines. Oh, where did those hairpins go?'

'Here, let me help,' said Rachel, scooping up the pins and deftly coiling Alison's curly hair. The girl looked very pretty indeed in the part of a beautiful society lady.

'You'll do just fine,' said Rachel, giving her a clap on the shoulder. 'And your folks will be proud of you.'

Rachel sounded so much like her old, friendly self that Alison steeled herself to ask hesitantly, 'Rachel, I haven't done anything to upset you, have I? Only you've seemed so distant the last couple of days.'

'Oh, Alison, of course not!' cried Rachel. 'I know that I've been acting a bit strange, but it's nothing that you've done, honestly. Look, we'll have a chat after the play and I'll explain everything to you. Now, come on – it's time!'

Then the lights went down, the audience fell silent and the curtains swished back. They were on! Rachel stood in the wings, fingers crossed as she watched apprehensively. For the past hour she had bustled around backstage giving a reassuring word here and a piece of advice there to the nervous actors. And how confident she had sounded! None of the third form had realized that Rachel was far more nervous than any of them, for the play meant a great deal to her. She watched the audience as much as the cast, looking for signs of boredom or restlessness. She found none. Everyone was absolutely enthralled. The lower school held its breath at the dramatic moments, while parents, mistresses and girls absolutely roared at Doris's hilarious performance. Mam'zelle was in the front row and her shrieks of laughter tickled everyone almost as much as the antics on stage. Mirabel was very good too, crashing around in her wheelchair, which she had learnt to manoeuvre most skilfully, while Gladys was just wonderful. Rachel spotted her own parents, saw her mother's eyes widen at Gladys's polished performance, then watched her whisper something to her father. Sir Robert, his eyes fixed on the small figure on stage, nodded agreement. Rachel guessed that they were praising Gladys and, where a short while ago she would have felt intensely bitter and jealous, now she felt absolutely delighted for the girl. Well, that just showed how a fine school like St Clare's could change attitudes!

At last it was over and the audience clapped and cheered its thunderous approval. Mirabel got an extra-loud cheer when she took her bow, still in her wheelchair, while Doris and Gladys both had standing ovations. But the loudest applause of the evening was reserved for Rachel who, at the insistence of the third formers, walked hesitantly on to the stage, looking rather shy. She felt that she ought to make some kind of speech, but found suddenly that there was a big lump in her throat which made it quite impossible for her to say a word, especially when she looked towards her parents once more and saw their faces glowing with love and pride.

'Three cheers for Rachel!' called out Carlotta, and the

whole audience joined in, almost raising the roof. Then the cast tripped off stage to change and remove their make-up.

'What a great night this is!' said Bobby happily.

'And the best part is still to come,' said Hilary. 'The after-show party! I don't know why, but acting always gives me a tremendous appetite!'

The others heartily endorsed this, making haste to get back into their own clothes.

'Wait a bit, Alison,' said Rachel in a low voice as the others made their way to the dining-room, where supper for the third formers and their parents had been laid out. 'Let's have that talk before we join the party.'

'All right, Rachel,' agreed Alison, looking at the girl curiously. 'Something has happened, hasn't it?'

Rachel nodded. 'I've wanted to tell you for days, but I was afraid you would be upset. You see, I shan't be returning to St Clare's next term. I'm going back to my old drama school.'

'But, Rachel, I thought you had given up all idea of becoming an actress,' said Alison, torn between surprise and dismay.

'I have,' replied Rachel. 'But Mum found out that the school is starting a new course next term, specializing in writing, directing and the technical side of things. Oh, Alison, I'll miss you terribly, but I've thought things out and decided that this is what I really want to do.'

Alison said nothing for a few moments, looking down at the floor. She was very upset, for she had grown extremely fond of Rachel. But she was not quite so silly and selfish as she had once been, and she knew that her friend had to take this opportunity. Alison certainly wasn't going to spoil their last day together with tears, so she lifted her chin, smiled bravely and said honestly, 'I'll miss you, too, Rachel. But I'm really thrilled for you – and we can write, and perhaps meet up occasionally.'

'That would be great!' said Rachel, pleased at the way Alison had taken the news. 'In fact, Mum said I could ask you to come and stay with us for a week during the holidays. Would you like to?'

'Oh, of course!' exclaimed Alison, delighted. 'That will be just marvellous! Now let's go and find your parents so that I can thank them for the invitation myself. And they must be just dying to congratulate you on your play.'

My play! How good that sounded, thought Rachel. And if it wasn't for St Clare's, she might never have discovered this hidden talent in herself.

22

Home for the holidays

'Rise and shine, sleepyheads!' called out Pat, as she awoke next morning. 'The holidays start here!'

One by one the girls sat up, excitement making them throw off their usual early-morning sluggishness as they realized that it was the end of term.

'And what a term it's been,' said Hilary.

'Yes, it's certainly had its ups and downs,' remarked Isabel. 'The ups, like our trick on Mam'zelle, and the play last night, were just brilliant.'

'But the downs have been dreadful,' said Pat with a grimace. 'There was all that horrid business with Fern, then the rift between Carlotta and Janet. Thank Heavens it's all sorted out now.'

'We shall miss Libby,' said Bobby. 'And Rachel. Funny how none of us was keen on her at first, except for Alison, of course, but she turned out to be a really good sort. It was quite a shock when she announced at the party last night that she wouldn't be back next term.'

'Well, I'm really pleased for her,' said Janet. 'And I hope that she makes a success of this new course. She certainly deserves to.'

The others agreed whole-heartedly with this.

'I must say, I thought Alison took the news very well,' said Isabel. 'This hasn't been an easy term for her. First she had to face up to the fact that Fern wasn't all that she seemed, and now she's to lose Rachel.'

'Poor Alison,' said Pat. 'Still, I think that Rachel inviting her home in the holidays softened the blow a little.'

'I wonder who your cousin will find to worship next term?' said Hilary drily.

'Don't even joke about it!' said Pat with a shudder. 'Oh, look at the time! We'd better get a move on. Our parents were going to a hotel in town after the play last night and they promised to get here early.'

'Mine too,' said Bobby, beginning to throw things frantically into a suitcase.

'Well, I don't think they'll be too pleased if you take this guy home with you,' chuckled Isabel, removing one of the school cats, which had sneaked unseen into the dormitory and lain down in Bobby's case for a snooze.

Extremely cross at being disturbed, he mewed grumpily at Isabel and went off in search of peace.

In the dormitory next door, Carlotta had finished packing when she heard her name being called from outside. Going to the open window she looked out. There on the lawn stood Libby and Will – with Rocky!

'Come down for a minute, Carlotta!' called Libby. 'We've come to say goodbye.'

Carlotta sped down the stairs and out through the front door, where she went straight up to Rocky, flinging her arms about his neck.

'Rocky wants to apologize for hurting you,' said Libby. 'I wasn't sure that you would want to see him, but Will said that you would.'

'Of course I do,' said Carlotta. 'What happened certainly wasn't his fault. Hey, Libby, you must be so excited about going to America after the holidays.'

'You bet! I shall be staying at a big ranch, you know, and helping out with the horses,' answered Libby.

'How marvellous!' exclaimed Carlotta. 'It's all going to be very different from St Clare's.'

'I'll miss being here, though,' said Libby seriously. 'I never expected to settle in so well – or to make such a good friend.'

'Here! You two aren't going to start howling, are you?' put in Will, looking alarmed. 'Because if you are, I'm off!'

'Of course we're not!' said Libby indignantly. 'Oh, I almost forgot! I have something here for you, Carlotta. It's from Fern. Her parents are coming to fetch her later, and Mum intends to have a serious talk with them.'

Carlotta took the piece of paper that Libby held out to her and unfolded it. This is what it said:

Dear Carlotta,

I am so pleased that you recovered from your dreadful accident, and am terribly sorry for the way I behaved towards you. I would not have been able to forgive myself if you hadn't got well again, and I just hope that you can forgive me. Libby told me that the play was a great success and I am glad of that as well. Please give Rachel my congratulations and tell her that I'm sorry for being so horrible to her too. I see now that it was my stupid jealousy to blame, and I mean to work really hard at conquering it, because I really have learnt my lesson.

Best wishes,

Fern

'Well, perhaps there is hope for her, after all,' said Carlotta seriously.

'She's certainly behaved a lot more sensibly just lately,' said Libby. 'If only she can keep it up.'

'We'd better be off, sis,' said Will. 'We promised Mum that we wouldn't be long. Carlotta, you will still come over for a ride now and then next term, won't you?'

'Try and stop me!' answered Carlotta with a grin. 'And, Libby, I shall expect lots of postcards from America. Have a wonderful time! Goodbye! Goodbye, Will – and Rocky!'

The usual end-of-term bustle was much in evidence when Carlotta went back into the big entrance hall. Laughing, chattering girls were everywhere and mistresses did their best to keep some kind of order.

'Jane, *must* you yell like that?' called Miss Jenks, the second-form mistress, in exasperation. 'And, Harriet, if I trip over your night-case once more, I shall . . . oh, I don't know what I shall do!'

'Ah, the dear girls! They are so, so excited,' said Mam'zelle. 'Soon they will be with their beloved parents again.'

'And we shall have a little well-earned peace,' said Miss Jenks dryly.

A group of third formers descended the stairs at that moment and Rachel called out, 'Mam'zelle, let me give you my address. You will write, won't you?'

'*Certainement*! I go to visit my family in France tomorrow and will send many letters and postcards. To you, Rachel, and Doris, and Hilary – ah, yes, even one to you, Janet, though you do not deserve one! All the tricks and jokes you play on me, you bad girl!'

'Well, Janet shan't be playing tricks next term, Mam'zelle,' laughed Pat. 'She won't be able to fool around once she's head girl.'

'Very true,' said Mam'zelle, nodding. 'She must – how you say it? – mind her ABCs.'

'You mean her Ps and Qs, Mam'zelle,' said Bobby with her cheeky grin. 'Goodness, I shall have my work cut out next term.'

'How so?' asked the French mistress, puzzled.

'I shall have to play *twice* as many tricks to make up for Janet,' Bobby replied wickedly. 'I must put my thinking cap on during the holidays and come up with some really brilliant ones.'

'*Non*!' cried Mam'zelle. 'There will be positively no tricks next term, Bobby, or I give you double French prep every evening!' But there was a twinkle in her eye and the third formers laughed. Then there came the sound of a car pulling up outside and someone opened the big front door.

'Parents!' called Doris. 'Hey, twins, they're yours.'

Quickly Pat and Isabel picked up their cases, saying their last goodbyes.

'*Au revoir*, Mam'zelle!'

'Goodbye, Rachel! Remember us when you're famous, won't you?'

'Goodbye, everyone! See you next term. Goodbye!'

Then the twins walked out into the sunshine and Pat said happily, 'Holidays! At last!'

'Yes,' agreed Isabel. 'But do you know what will be just as good? Coming back to St Clare's next term.'

KITTY at St CLARE'S

written by Pamela Cox

'I'm afraid our dear head girl is about to find out she's bitten off more than she can chew.'

New head girl Margaret has caused nothing but trouble for the third formers. Has she met her match in feisty Kitty and her pet goat McGinty?

THERE'S MORE TROUBLE at St CLARE'S!

CLAUDINE
at
St CLARE'S

Mam'zelle beamed.
'You will like the little Claudine!
For she is French.
She is my niece!'

But Mam'zelle is in for a SHOCK!
Out to break every school rule,
New girl Claudine is no teacher's pet . . .

THERE'S MORE TROUBLE
at St CLARE'S!

EGMONT PRESS: ETHICAL PUBLISHING

Egmont Press is about turning writers into successful authors and children into passionate readers – producing books that enrich and entertain. As a responsible children's publisher, we go even further, considering the world in which our consumers are growing up.

Safety First
Naturally, all of our books meet legal safety requirements. But we go further than this; every book with play value is tested to the highest standards – if it fails, it's back to the drawing-board.

Made Fairly
We are working to ensure that the workers involved in our supply chain – the people that make our books – are treated with fairness and respect.

Responsible Forestry
We are committed to ensuring all our papers come from environmentally and socially responsible forest sources.

For more information, please visit our website at
www.egmont.co.uk/ethical